The Battling Pilot

SELECTED FICTION WORKS BY
L. RON HUBBARD

FANTASY
The Case of the Friendly Corpse
Death's Deputy
Fear
The Ghoul
The Indigestible Triton
Slaves of Sleep & The Masters of Sleep
Typewriter in the Sky
The Ultimate Adventure

SCIENCE FICTION
Battlefield Earth
The Conquest of Space
The End Is Not Yet
Final Blackout
The Kilkenny Cats
The Kingslayer
The Mission Earth Dekalogy*
Ole Doc Methuselah
To the Stars

ADVENTURE
The Hell Job series

WESTERN
Buckskin Brigades
Empty Saddles
Guns of Mark Jardine
Hot Lead Payoff

A full list of L. Ron Hubbard's
novellas and short stories is provided at the back.

*Dekalogy—a group of ten volumes

L. RON HUBBARD

The Battling Pilot

GALAXY
PRESS

Published by
Galaxy Press, LLC
7051 Hollywood Boulevard, Suite 200
Hollywood, CA 90028

Printed in the United States of America.

ISBN-10 1-59212-305-8
ISBN-13 978-1-59212-305-6

Library of Congress Control Number: 2007903539

Contents

Stories from Pulp Fiction's Golden Age

A ND it *was* a golden age.
The 1930s and 1940s were a vibrant, seminal time for a gigantic audience of eager readers, probably the largest per capita audience of readers in American history. The magazine racks were chock-full of publications with ragged trims, garish cover art, cheap brown pulp paper, low cover prices—and the most excitement you could hold in your hands.

"Pulp" magazines, named for their rough-cut, pulpwood paper, were a vehicle for more amazing tales than Scheherazade could have told in a million and one nights. Set apart from higher-class "slick" magazines, printed on fancy glossy paper with quality artwork and superior production values, the pulps were for the "rest of us," adventure story after adventure story for people who liked to *read*. Pulp fiction authors were no-holds-barred entertainers—real storytellers. They were more interested in a thrilling plot twist, a horrific villain or a white-knuckle adventure than they were in lavish prose or convoluted metaphors.

The sheer volume of tales released during this wondrous golden age remains unmatched in any other period of literary history—hundreds of thousands of published stories in over nine hundred different magazines. Some titles lasted only an issue or two; many magazines succumbed to paper shortages during World War II, while others endured for decades yet. Pulp fiction remains as a treasure trove of stories you can read, stories you can love, stories you can remember. The stories were driven by plot and character, with grand heroes, terrible villains, beautiful damsels (often in distress), diabolical plots, amazing places, breathless romances. The readers wanted to be taken beyond the mundane, to live adventures far removed from their ordinary lives—and the pulps rarely failed to deliver.

In that regard, pulp fiction stands in the tradition of all memorable literature. For as history has shown, good stories are much more than fancy prose. William Shakespeare, Charles Dickens, Jules Verne, Alexandre Dumas—many of the greatest literary figures wrote their fiction for the readers, not simply literary colleagues and academic admirers. And writers for pulp magazines were no exception. These publications reached an audience that dwarfed the circulations of today's short story magazines. Issues of the pulps were scooped up and read by over thirty million avid readers each month.

Because pulp fiction writers were often paid no more than a cent a word, they had to become prolific or starve. They also had to write aggressively. As Richard Kyle, publisher and editor of *Argosy,* the first and most long-lived of the pulps, so pointedly explained: "The pulp magazine writers, the best of them, worked for markets that did not write for critics or attempt to satisfy timid advertisers. Not having to answer to anyone other than their readers, they wrote about human beings on the edges of the unknown, in those new lands the future would explore. They wrote for what we would become, not for what we had already been."

Some of the more lasting names that graced the pulps include H. P. Lovecraft, Edgar Rice Burroughs, Robert E. Howard, Max Brand, Louis L'Amour, Elmore Leonard, Dashiell Hammett, Raymond Chandler, Erle Stanley Gardner, John D. MacDonald, Ray Bradbury, Isaac Asimov, Robert Heinlein—and, of course, L. Ron Hubbard.

In a word, he was among the most prolific and popular writers of the era. He was also the most enduring—hence this series—and certainly among the most legendary. It all began only months after he first tried his hand at fiction, with L. Ron Hubbard tales appearing in *Thrilling Adventures, Argosy, Five-Novels Monthly, Detective Fiction Weekly, Top-Notch, Texas Ranger, War Birds, Western Stories,* even *Romantic Range.* He could write on any subject, in any genre, from jungle explorers to deep-sea divers, from G-men and gangsters, cowboys and flying aces to mountain climbers, hard-boiled detectives and spies. But he really began to shine when he turned his talent to science fiction and fantasy of which he authored nearly fifty novels or novelettes to forever change the shape of those genres.

Following in the tradition of such famed authors as Herman Melville, Mark Twain, Jack London and Ernest Hemingway, Ron Hubbard actually lived adventures that his own characters would have admired—as an ethnologist among primitive tribes, as prospector and engineer in hostile climes, as a captain of vessels on four oceans. He even wrote a series of articles for *Argosy,* called "Hell Job," in which he lived and told of the most dangerous professions a man could put his hand to.

Finally, and just for good measure, he was also an accomplished photographer, artist, filmmaker, musician and educator. But he was first and foremost a *writer,* and that's the L. Ron Hubbard we come to know through the pages of this volume.

This library of Stories from the Golden Age presents the best of L. Ron Hubbard's fiction from the heyday of storytelling, the Golden Age of the pulp magazines. In these eighty volumes, readers are treated to a full banquet of 153 stories, a kaleidoscope of tales representing every imaginable genre: science fiction, fantasy, western, mystery, thriller, horror, even romance—action of all kinds and in all places.

Because the pulps themselves were printed on such inexpensive paper with high acid content, issues were not meant to endure. As the years go by, the original issues of every pulp from *Argosy* through *Zeppelin Stories* continue crumbling into brittle, brown dust. This library preserves the L. Ron Hubbard tales from that era, presented with a distinctive look that brings back the nostalgic flavor of those times.

L. Ron Hubbard's Stories from the Golden Age has something for every taste, every reader. These tales will return you to a time when fiction was good clean entertainment and the most fun a kid could have on a rainy afternoon or the best thing an adult could enjoy after a long day at work.

Pick up a volume, and remember what reading is supposed to be all about. Remember curling up with a *great story.*

—Kevin J. Anderson

KEVIN J. ANDERSON *is the author of more than ninety critically acclaimed works of speculative fiction, including* The Saga of Seven Suns, *the continuation of the* Dune Chronicles *with Brian Herbert, and his* New York Times *bestselling novelization of L. Ron Hubbard's* Ai! Pedrito!

The Battling Pilot

CHAPTER ONE

Invitation—by Gunfire!

P ETER ENGLAND sat brooding over four throttles and a
wheel. His eyes went restlessly from left to right and
right to left, taking in a couple square yards of meter-studded
panel, watching oil temperature on Engine Three, revs on
Engine One.

A thin little fellow slid quietly into the copilot seat beside
him. England glanced in that direction with some annoyance.
"Huh. You're Tom Duffy. What—"

"On deck, Captain. I've been promoted to Number Ten,"
said Duffy, trying hard to hide his elation.

"Where's Nelson?"

"Sick list."

"You ever fly a kite?"

Duffy blinked. "Why, I've been copilot here for three years,
Mr. England."

"No time to break in punks. I've been on here for sixteen."

Duffy looked sideways with some misgiving. Pete England
was top pilot on the line, a long, hard-jawed devil, moody as
Atlantic weather.

"You bet," said Duffy. "Some day I hope to be tops."

"Don't," said England bitterly. "Nothing in it but grief."

"Grief? Why . . . I thought it was fun, scooting from New
York—"

"New York to Washington," said England. "Washington to New York. New York to Washington. Washington to New York. Lots of fun. You must be in a spin."

"Oh, no," said Duffy, his round face glowing. "I think it's swell. Keeping up the tradition—"

"Tradition," snorted England.

"Sure, tradition. You're the idol of—"

"Of what?" snapped England. "The passengers? Hell, you'll be telling me this job is romantic in a minute. La-de-da. You're a punk."

Duffy blinked and squirmed in the bucket seat.

"You're dumb," added England, as an afterthought. "A guy would have to be dumb to like this."

"B-But you're tops!"

"You've got to get on top to look back, don't you? Fun! What kind of fun is what I'd like to know. New York to Washington. Washington to New York. Flying a kite. Lugging sixteen passengers north for a lunch date, sixteen passengers south for a session with Congress. What kind of fun is that? I know every silo from here to New York. I know every spot on every cow. I can take a bearing on the number of milk cans sitting outside a gate. What's the fun about that?"

"B-But gee!" said Duffy. "You don't seem to realize what an honor it is—"

"To what? Cart sixteen passengers around, and half of them airsick? 'Mister Pilot, please don't hit the bumps so hard.' Damn the passengers. Maybe ten years ago this was romantic. But that was ten years ago. There was some element of danger then. Not now. This is as common as pushing a locomotive from Podunk to Punkin Center. If it wasn't for the pay, I'd have quit long ago. Say, what in hell is keeping those damned passengers?"

Duffy looked down the tunnel made by the awning and saw a group of people standing around the dispatcher. An argument was evidently in progress.

"That fat dame," said England, "is Mrs. Blant. She's going to see her daughter's wedding. She better put a waddle on or she'll miss the bells."

"Gee, do you know all of them?"

"There's a fellow there in brown I don't know," said England. "But the rest of them . . . That guy in the blue overcoat is sealing a construction job this afternoon and he's just about got time to make it. That young gentleman is Secretary Lansing's boy, on his way back—"

"Here comes a girl and an old dame," said Duffy. "Know them?"

Pete England leaned forward and looked across Duffy's uniformed chest. He scowled and shook his head.

"Nope," said England, "and what's more, we haven't got room for them. Boy, that old gal sure would break a mirror."

"The girl ain't so bad. Look there, Mr. England! If that isn't sable she's wearing, I'll eat it hair by hair."

"Probably rabbit," said Pete. "What the hell is Dan up to?"

The dispatcher was following the pair out to the ship. Above the mutter of the props, the pilots could hear the angry protest of the regular passengers.

"Now what in the name of the devil is this all about?" scowled England.

The dispatcher thrust his face through the door and balanced upon a wheel. "All right, Pete. On your way."

"All right hell," said Pete. "You sending me north empty?"

"You've got two," said the dispatcher.

"But what about Mrs. Blant?" said Pete. "Her gal's getting married this—"

"Never mind," said the dispatcher. "Number Six will hit here in about thirty minutes. We'll send Johnson right back with this bunch."

"You mean," said Pete, ominously, "that you'll gow up the whole day's schedule and maybe leave me overnight in New York just to send this dame and her grandma north? You're dizzy as a cuckoo clock, Dan."

"Never mind how dizzy I am. On your horse, Pete."

"She must be awful damned important," said Pete.

"She paid double for every seat in the ship. She's plenty important. Take it easy, Pete."

Savagely, England gunned the four throttles. The big kite rushed away from the awning, braked in a half circle, charged toward the end of the runway, whipped into the wind and stopped.

Out of habit, Pete swept his glance over the panel.

"Wait a minute," said Duffy.

"What the hell—"

A hand fell on Pete's shoulder. He turned and looked back into the cabin. Right behind him and looming over him stood the old lady. Her face was proud and haughty. She had the appearance of a battle-scarred general commanding troops in a charge. Her beady eyes drilled twin holes in England.

"I beg your pardon, sir," said the old lady, "but I must be quite certain that you are competent to fly this machine."

Pete gulped. He turned red. A blast of hurricane intensity almost left his lips. He swallowed it, choked on it and then managed, "Quite competent, I am sure, madam."

"I must see your pilot's license, sir."

Pete swallowed again. He dug angrily into his pocket and yanked out a compact folder stamped "Master Airline Pilot, D of C."

The old lady took it and carried it back to the girl.

Pete's view of the young lady was obscured by her companion's back, but he did see that the coat was really sable even at that distance. She was, he grudgingly muttered, a looker, damn her.

The old lady came back and handed Pete his license. "Her Highness is quite satisfied, sir. You may proceed."

Pete blinked at the title, but for a second only.

The old lady added in a wintery tone, "You will, of course, fly low and slow, sir. And please avoid the bumps."

"Yes, ma'am," gritted Pete.

The four throttles leaped ahead under his savage hand. The kite lashed down the runway, bit air, came off as lightly as a puff of smoke, streaked around to the north, climbing, and leveled out for New York.

"She said 'Her Highness,'" said the awed Duffy. "Gee, Mr. England, you don't suppose she's royalty or something, do you?"

"I'd like to crown her with a crankshaft," vowed Pete. "There you go, Duffy. You was just sitting there yapping about how romantic this job was. Now see what's happened. Mrs. Blant will miss half the wedding. Old man Lord will probably lose the construction job. Secretary Lansing's son will probably miss his date. All because some damned dame comes in and overawes those punks in the office. What the hell right has she got to bust into our schedule, huh? My God, what does she think we're running? A trolley car service? We've got schedules to make. We've a tradition of service to maintain. We've never slipped on a run for two years, and now look what happens!"

"You better take up the slack in that wheel," said Duffy in a faint voice. "We're rocking all over the sky."

"Let her rock," snarled Pete. "Let her bump. I hope those two dames get so sick Mary will have to—"

"Say, Mary isn't here," said Duffy, looking anxiously around at the cabin. "Gee whiz, what do you know about that?"

"Mrs. Blood-in-your-eye probably made them leave the hostess home," said Pete. "I never saw such a job in my life."

"Gosh," said Duffy, "I feel bad about that."

"Why? What's one hostess more or less?"

Duffy blushed and twisted. "Well, Mary and me were . . . That is, we thought . . . well . . . This was to be my first run with her and . . ."

"So you're the guy she's airsick over," said Pete. "Hostesses never were noted for having an overdose of brains. But she ain't a bad looker, Duffy. Not bad."

"She's wonderful," said Duffy, an ecstatic look in his big, baby-blue eyes.

"Nuts," said Pete. "Sure she's got the looks, but once you get

8

a dame tangled up in your controls, look out. It takes women to make trouble in this world. Now look what's happened here. This doll-faced babe throws around a lot of bunk about royalty in the office back there, and the boys fall for it. They disappoint sixteen regulars just to give this dizzy blonde a solo to New York. What's she want to get there for? Hairdressing appointment, probably. Maybe not even that important. But she's too good to ride with the common herd. Too high and mighty to make a reservation. Not her. She's got to bust the hell out of records and traditions, she has."

"Aw, she couldn't be so bad as that," protested Duffy. "Besides you just said you didn't give a fare-you-well about records and traditions. You said . . ."

Caught and caught fairly, Pete reddened, clamped his teeth together and made a hard, rough sound like a frozen piston.

The kite hurled northward, over the rolling green of Maryland, over stone walls and white houses, over big barns with false windows painted in them, over hills and valleys, chased on the ground by a shadow which accomplished prodigious leaps and twists.

Pete England let her rock. The ship had plenty of dihedral and could right herself. Why bother just to make a couple of damned dames comfortable?

The Maryland line was crossed. The squarer, cleaner farms of Pennsylvania fled behind them. A small range of hills loomed ahead.

Pete began to growl again. This was the first time in his life he had really been angry with a passenger, although he spent plenty of his time damning passengers in general. Somehow

9

his pride was touched, and that could not be accounted. He felt outraged.

His father had been a war pilot and had later pioneered the airways, incidentally teaching Pete to fly. Pete, starting his own career at an early age, just at the time the old flying circuses were folding up forever, had started on airlines. He had stayed with airlines and regular money and regular runs, and he rabidly stated that the only difference between himself and a locomotive engineer lay in the difference between overalls and a gold braid uniform.

He had, in short, no pride of profession whatever. The thing was as common to him as a cirrus to the sky. Eight years he had flown a steady schedule without a break. He did not realize the inconsistency of his present bitterness.

More than once he looked back at "Her Highness." The girl was young, about twenty-six, perhaps. She had a regal way about her, a well-bred composure. She was, as Duffy said, beautiful. Her hair was a yellow-blonde color. Her eyes were kindly and deep. Her mouth—

Well, damn her anyway for being beautiful, muttered Pete. And he promptly found new reasons to hate her.

The big transport plane was over the hills now, along a deserted stretch of sky and earth. A clearing appeared now and then below. Abandoned farms, left because of the weather's severity and the lack of adequate flat fields. Pete knew them all, one by one.

"Look," said Duffy, bumping Pete's arm.

Pete looked in the direction of Duffy's pointing finger. A single ship was yowling down the sky from the north.

"One of those damned Army pursuits on our beam," said Pete, banking slightly to get out of the way. "They're blind as bats. Last week when we had that fog I almost plowed right into one. He was flying his instruments, head down in his pit—"

"That isn't an Army plane!" stated Duffy. "It's changed its course for us."

Pete steepened his bank. The transport shot off its course to the right.

The approaching pursuit was coal black, sleek and fast, looking like it meant business and lots of it.

Pete scowled terribly, came around off his course and started north again.

The pursuit ship flashed down over them with a screaming engine, came up in a loop, banked and lanced by in the opposite direction.

"He's nutty," said Pete, a little pale at remembering the fatal playfulness of a pursuit pilot years before. A transport had been downed by a collision. . . .

A staccato rattle sounded above the droning transport's motors. Straight black streaks fanned out just ahead of the nose.

Duffy gaped at the streamers as they broke and whipped into the slipstream.

"Tracer bullets," said Pete.

The pursuit ship raced before them. A black-hooded head showed in the cockpit. A black arm pointed emphatically down.

"Say, am I dreaming?" said Duffy. "Is this the Western Front or is it the New York–Washington run? Are we a transport or a bomber?"

"Don't ask me riddles," snapped Pete. "That baby means business."

"We don't carry anything worth swiping," wailed Duffy. "The guy's nuts!"

The pursuit whipped around, bored straight up, flipped over and yowled down at them. The rattle sounded again. Black smoke trailed behind the bullets, making a momentary rail fence around the big kite.

The black arm was raised when the small plane ripped past them again. A black-gloved hand was patting a machine-gun breach with great promise. The emphatic gesture was final.

"There's a two-by-nothing field down there," said Duffy. "Right there by that old brick farmhouse. He wants us to land in it."

"Good God," said Pete, "I can't set her down in that! He won't dare shoot us down. Number Six will be over here in thirty-two minutes, and he knows the wreckage would be spotted. Shoot away, you damned buzzard."

It was as though the strange pilot heard the command. Glass went out from in front of Pete's face. The wind blasted in at him, cold on the small red cuts about his eyes.

Duffy snatched his wheel and righted the transport. Pete shook away the red film of blood and grabbed the wheel back.

A musical but afraid voice rang in Pete's ear. "Land! Land! They'll shoot you down if you don't."

Pete looked up at the girl. Fear was there on her face, almost hidden by a mask of ice, but not quite.

"You know that gent?"

"No, but . . ."

Pete snatched at the radio switch and bore down on the key fastened to the control column.

"Washington, Washington," rattled the key.

Blam!

Engine One leaped out of its mount and hurtled earthbound, prop splinters whined into Engine Two.

The shaken transport staggered in the air. Pete grabbed the wheel in both hands. He threw the switch on Engine Two and cut it. The black ship was coming around again. Tracer was lacing the sky in front.

Pete could do nothing else. He had both hands full. Duffy tried to get at a key and suddenly realized that he had no juice for sending.

Pete sideslipped back toward the brick farmhouse.

Wires screamed. The bottom fell out of the sky. The transport flipped level, nosed down.

Trees cracked the undercarriage.

Pete cut the guns and hauled back on his wheel.

The transport whistled down to a ragged landing on the rough terrain.

Pete braked into a ground loop.

He could hear the old lady saying, "There, there, dear. I know you tried. But this isn't the end. Somehow we'll succeed."

Men were running forward from the house with drawn guns.

Trees cracked the undercarriage.
Pete cut the guns and hauled back on his wheel.

CHAPTER TWO

While Transports Fly Over

THE black pursuit ship streaked back to earth and jolted to a stop. The pilot was out and running almost before the wheels had ceased to roll.

He shouted to the eight men who came from the house, but his language was strange to Pete and Duffy.

Scowling, dark faces appeared on both sides of the cabin. The doors were wrenched open. The girl and the old lady were seized with rough hands and dragged to the ground.

Pete tried to resist, but a jabbing muzzle almost broke his spine. He and Duffy were passed like relay sticks into the hands of the crowd.

Everyone was yelling at once. The men fastened like leeches upon the transport ship and quickly shoved it toward a grove of trees. The man in the black helmet was making haste now with the pursuit plane.

A great woven mask of branches and leaves was spread back on the edge of the woods, disclosing a crudely constructed hangar. The transport was gobbled up. The pursuit ship was thrust inside. The camouflage was tied back in place.

Sweeping the two passengers and the pilots with them, the crowd hurried toward the brick farmhouse.

The girl was tight-lipped. Her head was back and her eyes

blazed with anger. The old lady tried ineffectually to thrust away the hands which held them.

Pete stepped into the dimness of the house. He knew the place from the air. The shutters hung dismally on broken hinges, many of the slats missing. The windows were gray with dirt.

But the inside was different. Soft rugs had been laid upon the old plank floor. Furniture of square, brutal design and covered with black leather held forth an idea of wealth, but small promise of comfort.

The place was larger than he had imagined it would be, consisting of some dozen rooms. A prosperous farmer had once owned this place, but he never would have recognized it now. It had the air of a prison or a palace—which complement each other for chill.

The man in the black helmet removed his gloves and goggles. His face was narrow, coming out to a sharp blade of a nose. His lips were so thin as to be no lips at all. A hairline mustache gave him a feline appearance. In a way he was handsome.

The girl was thrust into a chair. The old lady stood imperiously behind her. No one else sat down.

Two brutish men, hairy-faced, dressed in a sort of dark livery, shunted Pete England and Duffy into a corner and pinned them there with automatics.

The farmhouse was silent for a long string of minutes. And then a droning sound could be heard overhead.

Number Six was on its way.

Pete did not breathe. He looked fixedly upward at the ceiling as though he could see right out through the roof.

Duffy was panting like a small dog on a hot day.

Number Six grew louder and louder until it reached a spot exactly in the middle of the clearing. The engines did not falter, the drone did not die.

Number Six faded out, unconcernedly on its way to New York.

The feline gentleman smiled and paced up and down the rug. He stopped and did a mechanical right-face.

He said, "There—you see? They have not the slightest idea, gentlemen, and I do not think they will search this place. You there—the tall one. You can take your eyes from the ceiling now."

"Thanks," said Pete. "Maybe you don't know this country very well, sourpuss. They put guys in jail for stopping planes and trains over here. If you wanted to talk to this lady, why didn't you do it in Washington? I don't like to have my schedules broken, and I hate like hell to lose an engine. Think that one over."

"Oh, I have no doubt, my gallant pilot, that you are angry. But to ease your mind about escape, allow me to state that I greatly doubt its possibility. And now, if you will be so kind as to hold your peace, I have some business with Her Highness."

"He don't look like so many," said Duffy to Pete.

"He sure don't," said Pete. "It's too bad they stopped putting stripes on them. When he's behind bars, he'll look just like any other jackass."

"Gentlemen," said the man in black, severely, "If you would be so kind . . ."

"Rotten shot," said Duffy. "And a punk pilot. We ought to show him how while we're here, Mr. England."

"You can't make a—" began Pete.

"Emil!" snapped the gentleman in black.

Emil was evidently one of the guards. He grinned, showing a number of places where teeth had once been, blew garlic into the faces of the pilots and jabbed hard with his automatic.

Pete subsided.

"My dear Maritza," said the gentleman in black, "you might spare yourself considerable pain and trouble if you told us where it was."

"I cannot allow the princess to address you, Barin," said the old lady.

"Louise, you will please stay out of this. As you know, I have the upper hand everywhere. This last sad effort, under the cover of diplomatic passports, has failed miserably. We have watched you since your arrival in this country and do not now intend to be stopped by a wrinkled old crone. Maritza—"

"Barin," said Lady Louise, sharply, "may I remind you of your manners. Not that you ever possessed any, but I had hoped—"

"Your Highness," said Barin, "you may as well know now that you have failed. Even without it, your mission has come to an unhappy conclusion. Whether I obtain it or not, may I advise you that our forces are everywhere victorious. . . ."

The girl lifted her head, gave Barin a bitter glance. "You have not forgotten how to lie, Barin. You would not be here if you had the upper hand. You would not have tried such a thing as this. Your life is in great danger, whether you admit it or not."

"My life?" cried Barin, laughing with delight. "How she talks, Louise. My life in danger. And all I have to do is give the command and you are dead, both of you!"

"You will give no such command," said the princess. "A black jacket is not enough to hide a yellow skin, Barin. With this ill-advised move, you have quite destroyed yourself. Have the large plane rolled out of its place and repaired, that I may continue to New York."

Her tone, the air of competent command which hung like shining armor about her, gave Barin pause.

He recovered himself in an instant. A flickering gleam came into his midnight eyes.

"Constanza!" he called.

Footsteps were heard on the stairs. A woman, quite obviously Barin's sister, entered. Her hard, cruel face turned toward the princess. She smiled amusedly.

"You have come far," said Constanza, "but not far enough, Maritza. Come, must we coax you?"

"Touch her," cried the belligerent Lady Louise, "and you sign your death warrants."

"How now," said Constanza, "what is all this talk of death? Maritza, Your Highness, Barin and I have nothing but profound respect for you. We would never kill you. Not personally, Your Highness. Give us this thing and we shall leave you here, only under guard long enough for us to reach the Continent."

"I had a friend who once trusted you, Constanza," said the princess. "He died, mysteriously, with a knife in his back. I have not forgiven that, nor do I intend to forgive it. This impudent assumption of responsibility can only end now in two executions. I shall order it, I assure you, at the earliest possible moment. As for my trust, I am afraid that search will avail you nothing and I would thank you not to touch me."

Barin jerked his thumb in the direction of the door. "Maritza, if you go peaceably, perhaps I will not have to assist. You may accompany her, Lady Louise."

Realizing that she could gain nothing with stubbornness, the Princess Maritza, followed by her lady-in-waiting, stepped though the door and disappeared up a flight of steps.

"A real live princess," said Duffy. "Gee, Mr. England, I didn't think that they existed anymore."

"They will not exist very long," said Barin, smiling like a well-fed black panther. "Emil, take these two fellows into the wing bedroom and secure them there with a guard."

"You can't do that," said Duffy. "You must be dumb, mister. This is Pete England, ranking pilot of the ACA fleet. You don't know what you're letting yourself in for. The Army and the Navy and the Marine Corps would scatter you so wide they'd have to bury you in thimbles. I don't know what the game is, but by God, this is the United States of America and you've stopped a crack airliner, and whether you like it or not, you'll pay and pay plenty."

"Large talk," said Barin. "Come, Emil. Quickly."

"Your name," said Pete, "is Barin, evidently. I don't know who you are, what you are or what the big idea is, but I've got one thing to say, hotshot. When we get out of this—and don't think we won't—that pretty mustache of yours will be no more. I'm reserving the absolute right to pull it out hair by hair. Until then, sourpuss, happy landings."

Shoved along by the hairy Emil and his coworker, Pete and Duffy were hurried up the stairs, down a hall and into a high-ceilinged room.

A lamp burned on the table, because no daylight could enter through the blacked-out window. The furniture here was rickety and covered with dust.

The door slammed. A lock grated. A board creaked as Emil sat down outside.

Pete looked sourly at Duffy. "You damned jinx."

"Me a jinx?" gulped Duffy, offended. "Not me, Mr. England. It's that princess."

"All right, she's a jinx," said Pete. "What the merry hell is this all about?"

"She's got something these guys want," said Duffy. "Maybe it's the crown jewels or something like that."

"Crown jewels," snorted Pete. "There isn't a set of crown jewels left on the Continent. Say, that was a funny one."

"What?"

"That gent Barin talks some goofy lingo to all those men but he talks English to this princess. That doesn't make sense."

"Maybe they wanted us to hear it."

"They don't care what we hear," gloomed Pete. "We aren't going to live long enough to hear anything this side of A major on a harp. Those guys know what they've done. They've stopped an airliner, and that's just the same as stopping a train, with the added attraction that stopping an airliner is also attempted murder, when done with bullets. The Army will be out here combing these hills before dark, and they'll stand these guys up in front of a firing squad or something—"

"They won't know where to look," said Duffy. "I got a glimpse of three fellows coming back to those woods rolling Engine One. But we'll get out of here. All we've got to do is break that window, climb down, get to the ship, start it up—"

"Take off with two engines conked, play tag with machine-gun fire on the ground. . . . Nuts," said Pete England. "I never in my life heard of anything like this happening to a poor hard-working pilot. I've seen them smear in. I've watched them burn. But I never even heard of an airliner being yanked down out of the sky because it was carrying a princess. The minute that dizzy dame stepped aboard, I knew we were in for trouble, and zowie, here it is."

"She isn't dizzy," said Duffy. "She's beautiful."

"She's dizzy," said Pete with an air of finality. "What's the idea of sticking up for her? What would Mary think?"

"Mary . . . well . . . that's different. I didn't mean . . . You wouldn't tell Mary, would you, Mr. England?"

Pete walked in a circle around the room, looking like a caged lion. He kicked over a chair, thereby injuring his right foot. He stood in front of the fireplace and swore futilely.

Duffy sank down on the edge of the bed and held his chin in his hands.

A drone in the sky grew louder and louder, and then began to fade.

Number Eighteen had passed into the south, wholly

unaware of anything wrong below. Obviously Number Eighteen would know about the missing transport, but that pilot had a job to do, and he could only spare a worried glance as his contribution to the search. The route was too long for an inch by inch ground search.

Pete England's ship had dropped completely and utterly from sight.

Such things had happened before.

CHAPTER THREE

Pete England Makes a Promise

PETE'S long, hard frame was boiling over with resentment. Glaring at the fireplace as though the whole thing was the fault of that inanimate object, Pete silently cursed the cheerful Duffy, the beautiful princess, the seasoned and salty lady-in-waiting and the feline Barin.

Pete was under no delusions about his own standing, even if he got out of here. A record was a good thing to have in your pocket. It kept you eating when things got tough. And Pete's record was his meal ticket. Never a misstep had he made in eight years of flying. No crashes, no lost time. He was as close to perfection as a pilot can get.

And now this had happened.

Back in the office they would hang it all on Pete England's ears. They would be swearing in concert. Unless Pete could square himself positively and perfectly, even his job would totter and Pete England, ace of the ACA fleet, would have to tote Chinks over the border for a living.

As it is with a steamer captain, so it is with a pilot. No matter the circumstances, when a steamer hits the rocks, its captain may just as well get in practice stevedoring, because he will never have another responsible command. Past record has little to do with it.

To lose a transport plane in good weather was about as ridiculous as losing a bass drum in a parlor.

It was chilly in the old house. It was damp and musty. A fire, thought Pete, after a long while, would feel good. The kindling was there, all ready to go. Pete knelt on the hearth and took out a box of matches.

He remained staring into the opening and put the matches back. Voices were coming out of the chimney.

He edged forward, removed his cap and thrust his head inside. The voices were louder there, but before he could catch any words, he heard a door slam. Silence followed.

Curiosity and hope aroused, Pete pushed himself further inside. The old fireplace was made for large logs and, following the custom of days before central heating plants, it was evidently backed by another fireplace on the other side of the wall.

Pete went forward again and cautiously stood up in the gloom. His shoulders were a tight fit, but he squirmed and shrugged and finally raised himself high enough to look over a ledge and down to another hearth.

Above him was a patch of dusky blue sky, quite unattainable. Behind him was Duffy and his cloying optimism. Pete took a deep breath, hitched himself up, raised a damper out of his way and went over headfirst toward the other room.

It was a feat requiring a great deal of acrobatic skill. Pete, being a pilot and not an acrobat, let go too soon and landed on the other hearth in a shower of soot and cobwebs.

He rolled over and sat up.

Voices were coming out of the chimney.
He edged forward, removed his cap and thrust his head inside.

A gasp greeted him. The princess backed hastily away from the chair in which she had been seated and pressed herself against the wall, blue eyes wide and startled.

Pete superficially dusted his knees.

The princess recognized him.

Unhappily for her, Pete presented an amusing spectacle.

The princess laughed.

"What the hell's so funny?" demanded Pete roughly.

"Your . . . your face!"

Pete growled like a thunderstorm and stood up. A minstrel show end man stared back at him from a cracked mirror. Covered with soot, he very little resembled Pete England of ACA.

"Go on and laugh, you jinx," snapped Pete. "I didn't come over here to be a court jester. I came to see if I could help you out."

The princess sobered instantly. "I'm sorry," she said. "There's a pitcher of water and a basin."

"Thanks," said Pete glumly.

He washed his face and dusted his uniform, aware that she was watching him with a strange interest. When he had dried his features as best he could upon a pocket handkerchief, he faced her again.

"I suppose you're satisfied," said Pete.

"Oh, yes," said the princess. "You've done an excellent job. I can almost recognize you now."

"I didn't mean that," growled Pete, hating to be badgered even by such a beautiful woman as this one. "If you hadn't been so quick to show everybody how important you were by buying out Number Ten wholesale, this wouldn't have happened. I suppose you thought it was funny to leave Mrs. Blant and Mr. Lord back in Washington to miss their engagements in New York."

"I . . . Why, I didn't mean . . . I didn't think . . ."

"Of course you didn't think. What have you got to think with? I been on this run for years, and the first time I ever lose a ship any place is because you get smart and kid the office help that you're important. What do you think I am? A . . . a . . ."

"Lackey?" she said helpfully.

"Nuts," said Pete, unable to think of a better word.

"I know you must feel badly about your ship," said the princess, "but I am sure that I cannot allow such minor problems and considerations to worry me. I have more important things to think about, Mr. England."

"More important?" snapped Pete. "I suppose losing a fifty-thousand-dollar transport plane isn't important."

"I will be only too glad to reimburse your company."

"A lot of good that does. Talk is pretty cheap. You'll never get out of here to do that, if this guy Barin means what he says."

Her frostiness vanished. A flash of pain went across her face.

Pete was instantly sorry. He was not really angry about anything, he suddenly discovered. This lady was just a kid very much in trouble, princess or no princess.

"I'm sorry," said Pete. "Hell, I'm not worried about the price of the plane. They carry insurance on them."

"Very well," said the princess. "If you are not worried about it, we'll say no more about it, and if you can bear dirtying your face again, you can leave by the fireplace. There is a guard at the door."

"Wait a minute," said Pete. "Don't pay any attention to me. I'm all upset. Isn't there some way we can get out of this? Can't you hand over the crown jewels or something and get Barin to let you go?"

"Barin let me go?" said the princess. "That's hardly possible. And I might add that presenting him with . . . well . . . I can only say that such a transaction would only result in our immediate execution. Freedom does not lie in that direction, Mr. England."

"Pete is the name," said Pete. "I came over here to see how we could get out of this, and it looks like we're wasting time. If you could give me all the dope about this mess, I might give you a hand in bluffing it through."

"I'm afraid I am not at liberty to divulge my business, Mr. England."

"All right, all right. If you want to go regal on me . . . See here, Princess, if you'll tell me what the score is, maybe I really can help you out. You've got nothing but a washout to look forward to anyway."

She was silent for a long time, listening to the slow steps of a guard creaking up and down just outside her locked door.

Pete sank down in a rickety chair and watched her. She was good to look at. Her face, when she relaxed, was kind, and more than ordinarily pretty. She looked just like any other expensively dressed woman. Lugging a title, Pete decided, didn't make so much difference with a person after all. In fact, a small voice told him, if he didn't watch out he'd fall head over prop in love with her.

"You look honest," decided the princess.

"Yeah. Dumb, but honest," said Pete.

Another silence followed, and Pete was struck with an idea.

"Say, how is it you talk such good United States, Princess?" said Pete. "For a lady from Latvia or Lithuania or somewhere, you sure sound like an Iowa coed. Maybe," he hazarded, "you don't speak this Latvian or Lithuanian or whatever that lingo is."

She was startled out of her composure. Her glance was penetrating and questioning. Uneasily she said, "Are you guessing or do you know something?"

"Hard to tell," said Pete. "It's like weather. Sometimes you can guess it at a squint and do it right, and maybe the weather boys spend three days over their charts and guess it wrong. Now what is it? The crown jewels?"

"Listen, Mr. England. Please don't . . . I mean Barin would stop at nothing if he thought you knew anything. For your own safety, stay out of this. I have my country to think about, and the salvation of my people. I have a reason to die, but I have no right to ask you to risk your life for a cause you do not even understand."

"As bad as that?" said Pete. "There's only one thing wrong, Princess. A real hero doesn't lecture about his heroism."

She was startled again. She stepped toward him, glancing fearfully at the door. "Please. Please stay out of this."

Pete had an idea again. He smiled and stood up. He approached the fireplace and turned back.

31

"Honest," said Pete, "I don't know a thing about it, but I'll promise you this. If there's any way to get you out of here, I'll do it."

Their eyes held for an instant.

Quietly, she said, "I believe you."

Pete disappeared.

CHAPTER FOUR

But Barin Needs a Pilot

THE night passed peacefully, marred only by Duffy's restless grunts and moans. Pete had not had much sleep. He had spent the several hours thinking about the princess and about what a swell jam they were all in. But the more he had thought about the princess, the more he had wanted to help her.

Morning found Pete in an ambitious mood, but Barin put a period to hope.

Barin stood in the doorway, black-jacketed, his mustache newly waxed. He clicked his heels and gave tousled, hungry Pete a mocking salute.

"I trust your night passed comfortably," said Barin.

"Beat it," said Pete.

"And I trust you are quite rested?"

"Scram before I lose my temper," said Pete.

"Because," pursued Barin, ignoring Pete completely, "I have some work for you to do this morning."

"Me?" said Duffy.

"Both of you," said Barin. "After breakfast, you will accompany our good and trustworthy Emil."

Barin departed. Breakfast, such as it was, arrived. Pete and Duffy ate in thoughtful silence.

"He'll probably let us go today," said Duffy, with a cheerful smile. "He knows he can't hold us."

"Sure he does," said Pete. "A little bird told him."

"But he won't dare keep us any longer," said Duffy.

"Say," said Pete, "that guy will keep us if he has to use ice."

Emil, hulking and toothless, announced by a puff of garlic, entered. He picked his teeth with a pocket knife and leaned against the door. In his right hand he held an automatic languidly, and though the weapon was a Luger of vast proportions, it looked like a toy pistol in his mammoth grasp.

"We're being paged," said Pete.

They went out. Emil shuffled along behind them. The house seemed to be empty, except for the guard outside the princess' door. Duffy's spirits picked up. He began to whistle.

"Shut up," said Pete. "Just because you fly like one don't mean you can sing."

Duffy looked sad about it for a moment.

They went out into welcome daylight, and Emil shunted them along the edge of the trees toward the camouflaged hangar.

Two men were lounging outside a tunnel-like entrance. They stood aside to let the pilots pass. A moment later they were standing under the wings of the big transport plane.

Barin moved out of the shadows, smiling, apparently gracious.

"The motors are damaged," said Barin, "and I know that you gentlemen are quite capable of repairing them with the use of these few parts I have managed to procure during the night. You will please begin."

34

Pete looked at the new props and two cylinder heads and some push rods.

"See?" said Duffy, meaning that he knew all the time Barin was going to let them go.

"I don't see anything," said Pete. "Look here, Barin, if you think I'm sap enough to work over this ship for you, guess again."

"Oh, I rather think you will," replied Barin smoothly.

"And if I don't?" snapped Pete.

"Emil!" said Barin sharply.

Emil grinned. He reversed the Luger, gripped it by the barrel and hefted it slowly. Barin picked up a wad of cotton waste and handed it to his guard.

With great care Emil wrapped up the butt of the automatic and then, with a grin of anticipation, advanced.

Pete, glaring, stood his ground. Duffy let out a small yip of terror and backed up. To Duffy, Emil looked sixty feet tall.

Barin said something Pete could not understand. Emil looked disappointed, but he kept advancing.

Pete retreated three steps. His heels clanked in the pile of cylinders and push rods and wrenches.

Emil raised the Luger, snatched hold of Pete's arm and struck.

The padded butt thudded cruelly into Pete's face. Blood spurted. Pete went down like a felled tree.

Emil, grinning, reached over to strike again.

With a sudden movement, Pete went sideways, rolling. He came up on his knees. In his hand he held twelve inches of spanner, bright, hard and lethal.

But it happened too fast for Emil's slow wits. Before the giant could straighten, Pete lunged. The spanner clanged on Emil's thick skull and bounced.

Pete shifted and hit a second time. Emil folded up like a head-on crash.

The hangar swarmed. Duffy tried to cover Pete but he was swept aside. Barin stepped back. The guards closed in like a wolf pack.

Pete tried to strike, but they had his arms. They bore him to earth, covering him with blows.

"Enough," said Barin, cool and comfortably aloof.

The men stood up and back from Pete's unconscious body. Barin took a fire bucket and threw the chilly contents in Pete's bleeding face.

Slowly and sickly, Pete managed to sit up. Barin booted him in the side.

"Enough of that," said Barin. "You will now begin work on this plane. I have need of it."

Emil was up. His shaggy face was contorted with rage. Only a determined command from Barin kept Emil from tearing the pilot to bits with his bare hands.

Pete had nothing to say. He appeared very beaten. He bent over the parts and tools and sorted them out, shaking his head from time to time to clear it of the incessant buzzing and the stabbing pains.

Duffy was solicitous, but he could do nothing. He went to work very quickly.

Barin left Emil on guard. The others withdrew watchfully.

Pete muttered, "We fix it, see?"

"You bet," whispered Duffy. "I'm working as fast as I can."

"It will take all day, without cranes or anything," said Pete. "Barin knows that. Watch yourself, don't let them see us talking. Tonight, we'll have a use for Number Ten ourselves. . . . And you wait until I get that baby alone in some dark alley. Get going, kid."

They did not enjoy their labors as mechanics. Their business consisted of flying and the feel and taste of grease was not at all to their liking. They knew, of course, how to go about it, but for years Pete England had not done anything more serious to a motor than listen to it purr.

But somehow they persevered under Emil's vengeful glare, and with the passing hours their backs and arms began to ache. The job was not to be done rapidly. Darkness came and they fumbled in the feeble beam of flashlights.

Added to their misery was the sound of planes overhead. As regular as clocks, every half-hour the ACA transports roared on their way either to Washington or New York. Help was up there within fifteen hundred or two thousand feet, but it might as well have been in China, for all the hope Pete had of rescue and escape.

It was midnight when they staggered back to the farmhouse. The place was silent and brooding and cold. On the table lay some platters covered with meat scraps and bread.

Pete and Duffy ate wearily, and when they had finished they were again aware of Barin.

The man was standing in the doorway, and had probably been watching them for some time.

"I suppose the transport will fly," said Barin.

"Yeah," said Pete, grudgingly.

Barin left them. Emil herded them to their quarters.

Duffy flopped down on the bunk and was instantly asleep. Pete sat for a long time staring into the dark, thinking.

The princess, Pete told himself, was sure in one tough spot. She was a good kid, too, even if she was a foreigner. Sincere, she was, ready to do anything to accomplish her mission—whatever it was.

He wanted very much to help her, but he did not know how to go about it, nor did he possess sufficient facts to work out a plan.

He held his aching head in his hands for hours, pondering his chances. At last, dejected and forlorn, he stretched out and slept.

But even sleep failed to bring him relief. All night long he had nightmares in which Barin and Constanza and the princess were all tangled up, and the princess was about to be killed and Pete England had to stand by helplessly and watch the thing done.

And because of his dreams, when he heard the angry buzz of voices in the next room, he could not be certain whether he was still dreaming or not.

At last, as his brain struggled up through the cobwebs of sleep, he realized that this was the real thing and that, according to a crack in the blacked-out window, this was morning—late morning, at that.

He slipped into his shoes and stood up. The sounds were coming from the fireplace and he stood on the hearth listening.

But the words were not clear, although he could distinguish the princess' clear tones plainly.

Pete ducked and inched into the chimney, up over the ledge, until he could see the other hearth.

Barin's feline snarls were distinct. "There is no use of this, Your Highness. You can deny, disclaim and condemn all you wish, but you do not seem to realize that no one here will help you, and that it is questionable if, unless you obey me this moment to the letter, you will ever again see more than the walls of this room."

Constanza's purring voice chimed in. "My dear, you are being very foolish. You do not seem to realize that everything has played into our hands very neatly. There is no longer any need of your safeguarding—"

"Lies will get nothing from me," said the princess. "If you are victorious, as you claim, I do not think you would bother with this badgering. You will get nothing from me. How many times must I tell you?"

Barin's voice was low and threatening. "No more, Your Highness. Your family turned me out years ago. I need but little excuse to extract—"

"Barin!" thundered Lady Louise.

"Ah," said Barin, "you think I would not resort to coercion, eh? You think I have brought this piece of cord here just to whip at my boots, eh?"

There came the sound of a crash, followed by a scuffle. Then silence, save for Barin's hard breathing.

Pete went over the ledge.

The princess screamed in sudden agony.

Pete hit the hearth in a ball, rolled over and bounced up before Barin could whirl.

Barin had been tightening a cord around the princess' forehead with a stick. His hands were engaged for an instant.

Emil was there, but Emil's brain was seconds behind the events.

Pete grabbed Barin's shoulder and slammed a right into Barin's mouth. Barin went down across a chair, splintering it.

Emil's automatic was caught in his sash. That gave Pete an instant's advantage.

Pete grabbed up an andiron beside the hearth. Emil dodged, but the solid iron bit deep. Emil crumpled.

Barin was straightening himself out. Hand on his gun butt he came to his knees, sparks spraying out of his eyes, teeth clenched, white as paper with rage.

Barin fired.

Pete had beat the trigger by a half second. He fell behind Emil, grabbed Emil's automatic and leveled it across the monster's chest.

"Drop it," snapped Pete.

For an uncertain instant, Barin looked as though he would obey. But Pete had forgotten that his back was to the door.

The princess cried out a warning.

Pete rolled. He stared up into the muzzles of drawn guns in the doorway. Barin stood up and straightened out his dark jacket with small, angry tugs.

"Take that fool down to the basement," he ordered. "And don't bring him back!"

40

Pete got up. He looked speculatively at the automatic in his palm and then, resignedly, he tossed it down on Emil. With a crooked grin, Pete looked at the guards.

The princess reached up and caught Pete's sleeve. She tried to say something, but could not. Her eyes thanked him.

Constanza stepped away from the wall. "Barin, you are being hasty. You have forgotten that the transport plane—"

"I've forgotten nothing," snapped Barin. "There is still that other fool. Bring him in here and I will show you."

A guard departed and presently came back with Duffy.

Jerked from his slumber, Duffy was rosy faced and innocent. His baby-blue eyes took in the scene with quick darts. He saw Emil unconscious on the floor. He saw Pete smudged and bedraggled. He saw Barin's slowly bluing right eye.

Pete, in his turn, looked at Duffy without much hope. The situation was clear. Barin knew that, as long as Pete lived, this exploit was dangerous. This was the second time Pete had attacked. Barin evidently needed a pilot for the transport plane and only one pilot. Duffy would do. Pete was not needed. They would shoot him, dig him a grave in the cellar and dump him in, and no one would ever know what had become of Pete England, ace of the ACA fleet.

Duffy looked embarrassed, as though he had been caught robbing a sugar bowl.

Barin said, "You are a pilot, are you not?"

Duffy blinked and looked at the floor. Pete held his breath. Duffy would state that he was, Barin would issue the order, and that would be that, as far as Pete was concerned.

"Pilot?" gasped Duffy. "Me?"

"You," said Barin.

"Not me," said Duffy, with an air of apology. "I'm the mechanic. We've got to have a mechanic riding the transports, you know, and so I get to ride with Pete England."

Pete took his turn at blinking. Barin would never swallow that. Barin would know . . . But then, how would Barin know the methods used in conducting a transport line in the United States?

"You're lying!" snarled Barin.

Duffy gulped and backed away. With all the innocence at his command, he yelled, "Not me! Gee, don't make me try to fly a plane! I'm scared to death. I don't know anything about it. I've been flying as a mechanic, but I couldn't take one off. Honest-to-God, don't make me fly it!"

Barin was halted in his tracks. He gave Pete a bitter glare. "Take him back to his room and mount a double guard over him."

The princess sighed with relief. Lady Louise gave Barin a haughty sniff of triumph. Duffy was still protesting that he was scared to death.

Barin faced the princess. "This is not the end, Your Highness. You will tire of balking me. Tonight we will change your prison. Tomorrow you will be far away from here. Whether you give it up or not, it will never be of use to your forces."

Barin gave Emil a kick in the side which brought the giant to life.

The guards led Pete and Duffy away.

Pete was conscious of the princess' eyes upon his back. It was a warm, pleasant sensation.

CHAPTER FIVE

By the Beacon's Flash

I T was an hour before dawn, a few minutes after Number Eight had passed south.

Transport Number Ten looked like some big 'saurus of the tropical ages crouching in the darkness. Men moved uneasily under the wings. Other men tugged and hauled at the camouflaged door of the hangar.

The princess and Lady Louise were hurried into the cabin. Pete was boosted into the pilot's seat. Duffy slid in beside him.

Everything and everyone was silent. Ghostly mists curled across the field, the only relief in the blackness. The world was still asleep.

Barin stood just behind Pete. "Start her up. The men will roll her into position for the takeoff. Don't try anything."

Pete fussed with the boosters. He was not very happy. He did not know where he was going, and he did not know just what kind of mechanics he and Duffy had been.

The engines barked into strident life. Pete eased his guns to idling and let off his brakes. The men under the wings began to shove, and the transport rolled sluggishly over the uneven ground.

They reached the trees. The men turned the ship into the faint wind. A smaller, darker shape was being rolled out and started. That was Barin's ship.

The camouflage was replaced, the house was shut up.

Barin stepped down to the ground and thrust a man toward the cabin.

Madness took hold of Pete. For an instant the ship had no guard in it. Pete acted.

He slapped all four throttles to the end of the trident. The startled engines banged into harsh activity.

The ship lurched and started to roll ahead.

Barin clawed for the wing, tripped and fell. His startled minions drew hastily back from the whipping blast of the slipstream.

The transport gathered speed. An automatic's cough was buried in the roaring of the engines.

The wheels went light, Pete eased the stick back and the plane was light and swift in the black night.

Duffy was sitting with his mouth open. Pete was grinning savagely.

A small pair of hands gripped Pete's shoulders and the excited princess cried, "You've made it!"

It appeared, for the moment, that they had. Barin's ship was lost behind them. It would be hard to pick them up in the blackness. They had a dozen places near at hand where they could land in safety, and Barin had none.

Pete's grin opened into a laugh. He looked sideways and kicked his rudder so that he could see back for an instant. His laugh was snapped off short.

Directly behind them was a pinpoint of red. An exhaust from a single engine. It was as bright as a drop of blood in the ebon sky, and growing brighter.

The transport was plainly marked by four such exhausts, brighter because they blared to the rear.

Another spark appeared above and to the right of Barin's exhaust. A high-pitched, snapping sound came into being.

The transport lurched. Bullets were eating into the left wing. The right wing slowly began to rise. The ship staggered. With no more aileron left, Pete tossed the wheel to Duffy.

"There's an emergency field down by the highway," yelled Pete. "Land her there!"

"What are you going to do?" cried Duffy in alarm.

"Even her keel. Head her down. Buckle your belts back there. She'll be rough."

Barin's black ship shot over the transport and circled back.

Pete slid out of the door and to the wing. The wind grabbed at him and tried to hammer him off into the blackness.

In the cabin, by the light of the panel, he could see the princess. She had not moved from behind the pilot's seat. Her hands were convulsively gripping the leather back. Her eyes, wide and strained with fear, were fixed upon Pete's wind-ruffled hair.

Something happened to Pete's heart in that instant. She was not looking at the black plane and the red exhaust which swept down upon them. She was looking at Pete. She was not afraid of what would happen to her, but what would happen to him.

Ahead the restless white tail of a beacon threshed at the sky, blinking white, red, red, red, white, white, red, red, red . . .

Pete inched himself along the curved surface of the wing, holding hard to the leading edge, the motor mounts, anything.

His weight would be very small help in itself, but combined with full aileron, there was a chance of keeping the ship on an even keel long enough for it to land.

Barin was angling watchfully. He was convinced that the transport was about to land, and he had no wish to crash it. Killing was not Barin's game just now.

The emergency field was small at best, poorly lighted, marked only with the beacon. But a faint pearliness in the east was helping Duffy out.

With Pete at the extreme end of the wing and with his weight acting there as a lever to keep them level, the ship coasted down toward a landing.

Barin hovered over them, and then banked away to race out and get in position for a landing of his own. As Barin was armed, he would experience little difficulty in recapturing his game.

The emergency field was deserted. The nearest house was a thousand yards away. It was not likely that the descent of the transport would, silent as it was, make the countryside turn out.

Pete clung to the wing, sprawling precariously upon it. He saw the beacon grow taller and taller before them, until it was higher than the plane, until the beam no longer hit them.

Duffy was juggling the sluggish controls. Without aileron play, he had no way of sideslipping in, and killing speed and height.

They were a little to the right of the runway and turning further still. The wing was doing that. Duffy was fighting the transport as straight as he could.

The runway raced under them. The wheels touched and rebounded. They were going too fast and would carry too far. But Duffy could still ground loop.

Again the wheels touched and stayed on. A row of trees, straight and forbidding in the gray light, rose up before them. Pete shut his eyes tight.

Duffy braked cautiously. The plane swerved and Duffy let up an instant. He threw the wheel hard over and tromped his rudder.

The transport came around like a whiplash. One wing grazed the trees. Pete felt a stinging blow on his shoulder. His grip loosened. Like a pebble from a slingshot, he was catapulted into the brush.

Stunned, he lay still, and the transport headed out, undamaged, in the other direction.

Barin had been able to slip down swiftly. He bobbed out of his cockpit, gun drawn, and sprinted for the big ship.

There was no thought of resistance now. Duffy docilely opened the door and looked out. He had not yet missed Pete. He had not even seen Pete since Pete had left the cabin.

Barin leaped up on a wheel, black hooded and jacketed, like some night prowling falcon.

"Where is the other one?" demanded Barin.

Pete heard that, although he was two hundred yards away. He came groggily to his knees and stared.

The princess answered. "He climbed out on the wing and fell. He tried to right us when your cowardly—" Her voice broke there, and Pete felt good about it and sorry for it all at the same time.

47

Barin poked into the cabin, and then faced Duffy again. "You lied to me. You said you could not fly and yet you landed this ship. You can take it off again immediately."

"But the wing," protested Duffy.

"To hell with the wing. See here, connect this control wire and the aileron works. Swiftly!"

Duffy could do nothing else. Under the menace of Barin's gun he obeyed.

"I have no compunction about killing you now," snarled Barin. "You will take off and fly back to my field. You know that I can do that with ease. I can shoot you down with pleasure and gladness. And you, Your Highness, have played with me long enough. I know what you have. Somewhere about you you have hidden a Bank of England check for five hundred thousand pounds. I know that and I mean to have it. You do not dare destroy it because with its destruction the chances of your people in Rangaria would also be destroyed. I mean to have that money. Remember it. That fool of a pilot is dead and you can abandon the thought that he can save you. This time . . . But we waste precious minutes. Take off and watch where you fly. I will be behind you."

Barin backed toward his own plane, got in and kicked it into takeoff position.

The transport started up, going faster and faster until it took the air.

The black ship leaped away from the earth.

The combined engine roars dwindled to silence.

Pete stood up and thoughtfully pulled thorns out of his face and hands.

"A check for five hundred thousand pounds," he muttered. "Good God, no wonder that bird is so hellbent on this thing."

He walked toward the highway and lifted a hopeful thumb to a lone motorist. The man stopped and Pete was on his way back to Washington, vengeful plans whirling through his head.

CHAPTER SIX

Trouble Hails All Around

I T was half-past eight when Pete England stepped out of a taxi before the Administration Building. The dispatcher gawped at him. The desk clerk's eyes widened and grew perfectly round. But Pete paid them no attention. He had important things on his mind, and it did not occur to him that to them he was a man returned from the dead.

He walked straight through to the office marked "Operations," went through that into the carpeted and draped sanctuary.

However, Brainard, the man who regulated ACA's destinies, did not come in until nine, and Pete had a half-hour before him. He looked down at his ragged serge, at his blackened hands, at his scuffed shoes and then felt his stubbly chin. He had a change of clothes in his locker, and he used the half-hour in preparing himself.

When he had finished, Brainard was ensconced behind his mahogany, looking very fierce under his upright shock of gray hair which bore every resemblance to steel wool.

Brainard was not a man to be startled. He offered Pete a chair and a cigarette.

"All right, England," said Brainard, "shoot—but don't strain your imagination. I'm perfectly willing to listen impartially, but I'm telling you before you begin that you have an awful lot to explain."

Pete started. He went full gun through his tale of woe and worry, and did not pause until he had finished with, "And so here I am. Number Ten is still airworthy, Duffy is probably still alive, but neither of them will be unless we do something and do it quick. You yaps in the office here sure played hell when you gave me a princess for a cargo."

Brainard smiled in a mysterious way. He drummed the desk with his nails and looked sideways at Pete.

"I would like to believe you," said Brainard, "but there is one thing wrong with your story."

"One thing!" cried Pete. "There's everything. But the whole thing is true, so help me! That's how I lost Number Ten and I—"

"Save it," said Brainard. "The one thing I have in mind is this Princess Maritza. There *is* a Princess Maritza, you know."

"Of course there is!" shouted Pete.

"But, unhappily for you," said Brainard, "she did not take off in Number Ten. The woman who went north with you announced herself as a Mrs. Sheldon."

"Of course she did. She was incognito, see? She—"

"The Princess Maritza," said Brainard slowly, "is right here in Washington."

"My gosh!" gasped Pete. "That's swell. But how... how..."

"To make everything clear," said Brainard, "we will call her at her hotel."

"Great!" said Pete.

Brainard put the call through and presently handed Pete the phone.

Eagerly, Pete said, "Hello. Is this you, Princess. How did—"

A foreign accent said, "Who ees thees, please?"

"Why, this is Pete England," said Pete, taken aback.

"I am sure I do not know you, Meestaire England." She hung up.

Pete knew it was all wrong. That wasn't *her* voice.

"See here," said Pete to Brainard, "this Barin guy has spotted that dame here in Washington to masquerade as the princess. He isn't missing any chances—"

"Now come on and tell me," said Brainard. "How much did you get for running off with Number Ten? Is this a publicity stunt to get this Sheldon woman in the movies, or what?"

"You really believe that I . . ." Pete sank back in his chair, looked at Brainard for several seconds and then abruptly bounced to his feet. "Damn you for a fool!" cried Pete. "We've got to act fast to get Number Ten back, if that's all that worries you. Call out the Army and the Navy. Get—"

"This is no case for anyone but a police officer," said Brainard, reaching for his phone again.

Pete stayed his hand. "Wait a minute, Brainard. You know in your heart I'm square. You know I wouldn't pull anything shady on you. Look here. I know the Army won't do anything, but like all us guys, I've got an Army Reserve commission. I can get a ship at Bolling, get back up there to Pennsylvania and stop this Barin from doing anything else. You can call the State Police in Pennsylvania, give them my directions, have them check me up, and we'll have everything shipshape in a matter of hours. This princess at the hotel is a phony. I know what I'm talking about."

Brainard looked dubious. In the balance he had a transport ship worth tens of thousands of dollars. He had an astoundingly wreck-free record to maintain. He had no real grounds for thinking Pete was acting in somebody else's pay.

"Okay," said Brainard. "Okay. I'll ring Bolling and back you. But get this, England. If you don't show me that what you say is truth, you'll have a lot to explain before both the Department of Commerce and the civil authorities. Many men would pay you for pirating a ship. South America needs our transports for bombers. I've had offers for our old crates more than once from that source. You better come back here with Number Ten or you'll come back wearing bracelets. That's all."

Pete left. He had been annoyed before. He was mad all the way through now. A small voice in him said that Brainard was just putting him on his mettle, but Pete's anger rode the voice down. What charge could they place against him anyhow?

Theft.

Maybe even murder, if Duffy was killed by Barin and if Duffy's body was ever found.

Pete had something more than Brainard's threats to egg him on. He had to haul Duffy out of the mess, of course. But he had to see the Princess Maritza again.

The way she had looked at him when he had gone out on that wing still made Pete's heart feel funny.

On his way to the taxi lines he saw the girl Mary hurrying

across the terrace to meet him. He didn't want to have to tell her what a mess Duffy was in. He dived into a cab and ordered the driver away.

He had a great deal on his shoulders. A great deal more than he cared to think about. Instead he thought about the princess.

It occurred to him as he rolled down Pennsylvania Avenue toward Anacostia that the Princess Maritza was, after all was said and done, a princess. And he was just a pilot. Quickly he banished the thought, but it had shaken him not a little.

At Bolling he was able to shake off his nagging thoughts by diving into action.

Pete talked first. As an Army reservist, he was entitled to consideration in the way of ships, but when he started to beg for machine guns and when the ordnance officer heard his pleas, objections began to rise all around him.

And then Brainard phoned. Brainard had quite a bit to say about this and that politically, and he said it.

Pete got a pursuit ship, with a machine gun on it. He got a .45 Colt automatic.

And then, armed and girded for war, he hunched down behind the little plane's shield, gunned the mighty engine forward and charged across the field and into the morning air like a silver lance thrown skyward.

Barin, thought Pete, had better oil up and fly hard and fast if he wanted to keep out of trouble now.

CHAPTER SEVEN

A Completely Baffled Pilot

PETE flew the route and flew it faster than he had ever flown it before. The single-seater, a stubby-winged, snarling ship, built to deal death and destruction, was like a bullet under his throttle hand.

In spite of Brainard's questioning attitude, the man had carried through. And now if Barin was still in Pennsylvania, Pete knew he would find him.

The Pennsylvania State Police would be on their way and would probably arrive a few minutes before Pete would get there. Pete was hoping that Barin would make a break for it. If he did, Pete promised himself that he would knock Barin spinning out of the sky. It would be a pleasure to match that black ship with one of its kind.

Pete, like almost all transport pilots flying the airlines, had had reserve training and he could, on occasion, play hell with gunnery and stunt tactics.

He had the wherewithal now. All he needed was a target like Barin would make against the smoky blue sky.

Maryland fled under his short wings and gave way to Pennsylvania, and the hills loomed up ahead.

Pete crouched forward tensely, hoping to see the black plane, but it was not in evidence. Barin was in for a surprise, gloated Pete. This was going to be too easy.

Suddenly the clearing was under him. He put down a wing and looked at the brick farmhouse.

The place was deserted, but Pete had expected to see the hangar closed and the house lifeless. Barin and Constanza and Emil and the rest would be inside, of course.

A movement showed in the trees. Pete circled and made out the snappy uniform of a State Trooper. The place was guarded from the ground.

Good.

Pete dived toward the trees, cut his gun and banked. He swooped down upon the field, made a matchless landing and taxied toward the house, his hand on his gun butt.

Let them try to get out now. Oh, for a glimpse of Barin.

Pete came to a stop. A trooper strode toward him. Pete stepped out of his cockpit, lifted the flaps of his helmet and said, "Have you got them already?"

"Who?" said the trooper. "This place is empty, brother."

"Empty!" cried Pete. "But you haven't been in the house . . ."

The doorway filled for a moment and two more troopers came out. One of them, a corporal, looked thoughtfully at Pete.

"We got a tip some kind of gang was here," said the corporal, "but somebody's crazy. There's dust all over the place. Hasn't been lived in for years."

Pete jumped down to the ground and walked confidently toward the trees where the hangar had been. He saw that something was wrong with the place. Then he realized that where the hangar had stood there was only a small clearing. No sign of the brush doors, or even of wheel marks on the earth.

The grass had been carefully lifted upright by hand. Dust

had been scattered carefully. Nothing remained to show that Barin had been there at all.

Panic-stricken at the thought of losing all touch with the princess and Duffy, Pete sprinted for the house. He dived in and went through it like a hurricane.

But not one single object rewarded him. The furniture was gone. The windows were dirty and scaly.

Pete came out and stalked toward his ship. His jaw was hard and his eyes were narrow.

"They've restored the place," said Pete to the corporal.

"Pretty good job—if they did, mister. We got orders to look it over, and that's all. They said something about a guy that was to fly up here, and I guess that's you. They said if we didn't find anything, we was to take you into custody, or something like that."

Pete looked at the corporal in amazement and then thought swiftly how he could escape.

But he had three big troopers between himself and freedom.

The corporal was still talking. "But they always give us screwy orders like that. We can't do anything about it because we haven't got a warrant and don't even know the charge. They must be crazy down at headquarters."

"They must be," said Pete, gasping weakly.

"Well, lots of business to be done," said the corporal. "So long, mister."

The troopers walked away, and presently motorcycles popped in the woods and faded out in the distance.

Pete sat down on a wing and held his chin in his hands.

Gone.

No chance of finding them now.

Barin was after a check, God knew why, unless it was just for the sake of the five hundred thousand pounds. But checks weren't payable to everybody.

Pete got up. He was remembering how the princess had looked at him, how her hands had clutched his shoulders. Even if he was just a pilot and she was a full-fledged princess, Pete permitted himself the fleeting pleasure of a dream.

He inserted himself into the office, reached for the gun and braked one wheel as he turned into the wind. His hand shot ahead. The little ship quivered and raced ahead, and took the air.

Someplace, somewhere, Pete would find her.

CHAPTER EIGHT

For Five Hundred Thousand Pounds

FOR eight years Pete England had flown from Washington to New York, from New York to Washington. Occasionally he made Richmond; now and then he did the local run and stopped at Philadelphia.

His course had been over the same ground, and he had rarely deviated more than five miles to either side of the beam. He had forgotten that the Atlantic States are, after all, fairly large and that the proverbial needle in the haystack was bigger than a smelter chimney compared to two airplanes with half a dozen states in which to land.

Furthermore, it was unlikely that Barin would stay on the airlines. The man would naturally hide all traces.

Pete was thinking fast. If he were Barin, where would he go? Certainly not north, because that way was studded with airliners and cities. Not south because he would inevitably be seen and he would naturally think that all eyes were searching skyward for a trace of Transport Number Ten.

With two points of the compass eliminated, Pete turned his thoughts to the west. It seemed good sense to go west, into the mountains. No trace of passage would be left in that direction. But, on the other hand, there were few enough landing fields in the Alleghenies.

Indeed, Barin would show poor sense to move away from his original base at all, unless he had some definite plan in mind. And any plan Barin might form would obviously be concentrated upon getting out of danger.

Pete began to see light. He headed the pursuit ship east.

That way lay a long, deserted coastline. Barin had come from Europe; he would, quite likely, head back again at the earliest moment. It seemed natural. The beach, except for Coast Guard stations, offered a long, untenanted landing field. A boat could anchor far out, as the rumrunners had done. Small craft could come in to shore, pick up passengers. The two planes could either be hidden or wholly destroyed.

If Barin worked progressively, he would try to get out to sea and out of the way of any and all searching parties.

A man, thought Pete, would go through a lot to get five hundred thousand pounds—considerably more than two million dollars. He would hardly risk his chances of obtaining that sum by dallying too long under cover or by exposing himself unnecessarily. Besides, Barin had done a lot of talking about a "cause," and so had the princess.

Funny that Barin had been unable to uncover that check prior to Pete's departure. The princess had had only a few places to hide it, and she would hardly leave it in the upholstery of the transport plane.

If Barin had uncovered that check by this time, Pete knew there was little use of his trying to find the princess, Lady Louise and Duffy still alive.

The pursuit ship's roaring engine bored air toward the

coast. Below, Delaware and New Jersey could be seen all in a glance. Ahead, the gray blue Atlantic began to shimmer in the noonday sun. Delaware Bay was a long triangle, checked by small waves, sticking like a steel wedge into the flats of the coast.

Shoving miles rearward every minute, the pursuit plane gobbled the distance. The surf was directly below, a long white line of chalk drawn between the gray dunes and the blue troubled water.

Pete banked to the north, away from the resort village he saw in the opposite direction. He came down to a thousand feet, leveled out and sent his snarling Pegasus like a shot arrow above the sand.

Straining his eyes in the slipstream, he studied the sea, watching for a boat. It seemed unlikely that Barin could evacuate the farmhouse, land on this coast, embark in a small boat and head over the horizon in a space of six hours. It would take time to repair that farmhouse, to land and wreck or hide the planes.

But only disappointment lay in the north. Abruptly the piers of Atlantic City stabbed black lines into the blue water.

Pete banked. The black bowl of his compass rocked and spun and finally came to rest on 200°.

The pursuit plane raced southward, back toward Delaware Bay. A lonely Coast Guard station fled below, momentarily cuffed by the plane's hurrying shadow. It occurred to Pete that he might do well to land and ask the Guardsmen if they had seen anything of two planes, but Pete was too panic-stricken at the thought that he might be wrong and that he had to make time.

Before he got to the bay, he passed over a long and uninhabited stretch of dunes just north of Cape May.

On a sheltered stretch of sand he saw two black dots. A ship was standing off about two miles from shore. A small boat was just putting in.

Pete swore with relief. He nosed down full gun and zoomed the place.

He was right. There was the black plane, there was Number Ten. And that bulk outside a weather-beaten shack was certainly Emil.

Pete hurtled skyward, did a wingover and dived again.

He was undecided just what he should do. If he tried to get help, he would have to leave the place. And it was quite apparent that within a few minutes that small boat would be on the beach and Barin would be loaded up and far at sea before Pete could return.

And neither could he rake the place with his machine guns. Men were running down there. Out in the sand, two guards were holding the princess. Barin was taking no chances of being shot up from the air. He had a hostage, and though he could have no clue as to the identity of his enemy, he could not mistake the red, white and blue fins of the pursuit plane, nor could there be any doubt, after Pete's dives, of his intentions.

Barin was no fool. He knew that he could not take off in the face of machine-gun fire in the air. And as long as he held the princess, he could still put to sea.

Pete had to take a long chance. He had to land. And once on the ground, his machine guns would count as nothing.

He banked around and cut his gun, whistling down for a crosswind landing.

Men halted in their tracks and stared upward.

Pete set down his three points and coasted toward the shack.

Before he had stopped rolling, he was out of the cockpit, .45 in hand. Using the fuselage for cover, he crouched and fired over the heads of the group.

A guard dropped to one knee and leveled a rifle. The range was about fifty yards, and though Pete was no marksman, he could not miss.

He fired, and the guard pitched over, tossing up a puff of sand.

Barin came out of the hut and ran up the side of a sand dune, dropping down over the crest before Pete could shoot. Emil sheltered himself in the doorway, sighted his rifle and seemed to be waiting for a signal.

A far, thin cry floated to Pete. It was the princess.

"Get back! They'll kill you!"

Although he knew that she could have no idea who he was, her warning made him feel good.

Another guard was trying to get into the cover of the dunes to shoot Pete on an angle. Pete shot first and the guard dropped slowly out of sight.

But the contest was as unequal as it was foolhardy. A moment later a black-garbed roughneck bobbed up on Pete's left and shouted something Pete could not understand. Pete tried to fire, but a shout on his right, on the other side of the fuselage, made him understand that he was about to be drilled from at least three places.

He had a sick sensation of knowing that he had but a moment left to live.

But for some reason, probably because they thought him an Army pilot, they did not shoot.

Barin shouted, "Throw down your gun and step out."

It was either that or be killed. Pete was forced into the open. Barin approached, stalking like an angry black panther. He came within ten feet before he recognized Pete.

"Ah!" said Barin, unwilling to show surprise. "You have returned to us, Mr. England."

Pete held his peace.

"A most foolish move," said Barin. "But come. We have little time to waste on you. Walk ahead, with your hands away from your sides."

Prodded by a guard's revolver in the small of his back and confronted by the grinning Emil and the sleek Barin, Pete walked.

Constanza came out of the shack. "Back again, Mr. England. So sorry you are not dead after all."

"Not now, but soon," smiled Barin, "eh, Emil?"

Emil did not understand the words, but he knew what Barin meant. He grinned.

The Princess Maritza would have rushed forward, but a man on either side of her held her back.

"You shouldn't have come," she said, her voice breaking.

"How could I stay away when—" began Pete.

Barin cut him short. "England, I have been somewhat foolish about you. I apologize. I thought you were merely an ACA pilot."

Pete waited.

Barin said, "I understand now that you must have been in the pay of Her Highness. We have searched very thoroughly, you know. We've torn the transport almost apart searching. We've tried a little bit of everything, and nothing seems to reveal the whereabouts of a small bit of paper of which I have need. You will please give it to me."

"Me?" said Pete.

"It was certainly in Her Highness' possession," said Barin. "It is obviously not in her possession now. I should have searched you when you were with us before. The item is, I might add, a check to the sum of five hundred thousand pounds. A cashier's check, made out to a certain firm in New York."

"Don't look at me," said Pete. "What the hell would I be doing with—"

"Emil!" snapped Barin.

Before Pete could jerk away, Emil had thrown him to the sand. Quickly Barin went through Pete's pockets.

There was little enough in them. Just his pilot's license and a wallet. Barin ripped the little black booklet apart.

Out fell a long slip of paper.

"How the devil did that get in there?" cried Pete, spitting sand.

"I'm sorry," said the princess. "I asked for your license in

Washington. I knew it would not be safe with me and—" The sight of Barin gloating over the check silenced her, and her apology to Pete shifted to rage at Barin.

The Lady Louise looked like an eagle about to pounce, but nothing could be done.

In great elation, Barin read the figures over and over. "To the Winton Arms Company too," said Barin. "And no signature necessary. Why, this is better than I had planned. No forgery, nothing. It is only necessary to give them this check, collect the munitions and, I promise you, Your Highness, royalty will have short shrift in Rangaria under Dictator Barin."

For an instant, Pete was almost glad that Barin had that check. If Her Highness lost out in Europe, then maybe a pilot would have a chance—

But instantly following upon the heels of that traitorous thought, Pete recalled his own position. Barin would hardly leave Duffy or Her Highness or the Lady Louise or Pete alive after this. The man was playing for stakes higher than Pete had ever dreamed of. Political ambition was far greater than a little murder. That check would finance Barin in a revolt against Rangaria's present rulers, when it had at first been intended to buy arms and ammunition for the protection against Barin.

No wonder Barin had followed the princess to the United States. No wonder Number Ten had been stopped, as it were, in midair.

Emil was looking eagerly at Barin.

Barin noticed him and said something in Emil's language. Emil looked speculatively down at Pete and flexed his big hands, groping for Pete's throat and muttering rumbles of pleasure.

A high and faraway drone came into being.

Barin glanced upward in alarm. Emil was distracted from his task and looked skyward.

Pete saw his chance. No matter what plane that was, for a moment eyes were aloft.

Pete bucked like a bronco. Emil was thrust sideways for an instant. Pete scrambled forward, and in his hand he clutched the Luger which had lately reposed in Emil's sash.

Emil dived for him.

Pete fired and rolled sideways. Emil thundered into the sand and lay still.

Sweeping the smoking muzzle in a half circle, Pete backed up, rising to his knees. Even then it was doubtful if he could get away with it.

Barin leaped backward and whipped at his belt. He stumbled and fell. Duffy had stepped out of the doorway and into his path. Duffy had Barin's gun in a matter of seconds.

Before the slow-witted guards could move, the princess herself had relieved one of the holstered Lugers and stood back with a level and steady hand.

The plane overhead was coasting in for a landing. The big letters on the side told their story.

The Coast Guard, ordered by Washington to be on the lookout for Pete, and having had a report from the station up the coast of shots and Pete's landing, had sent a big amphibian patrol plane to investigate.

And although the plane carried nothing in the way of

armament besides automatics, the sight of it thoroughly cowed the group.

An officer stepped out and roared, "What the hell is going on here?"

"I'm Pete England, of ACA," declared Pete. "Give me a hand with these guys."

The boat which had been heading in swerved to sea again. The officer stepped back and barked an order at his radioman, and presently sparks were flying in the big cabin.

"You don't look like you need any help," commented the officer-pilot with a grin. "What's this all about?"

"Well, I tell you," said Pete, "it's—"

The princess snatched at Pete's sleeve. "Barin! Don't let him get away with that check!"

Barin was gone.

Far down the beach, where the black plane stood, they could see him running. He had slipped around the edge of the hut and had escaped while hidden by the sand dunes.

The range was too great, and Barin was moving too fast. He reached into the pit, raced around to the prop and pulled it through. The already hot engine caught and roared into life. Barin leaped into the cockpit.

Pete was on his way. He had fifty yards to travel in the opposite direction, and when he got to the pursuit ship, he had to turn it and start it.

Barin was in the air thirty seconds before Pete started his ship rolling.

Pete jabbed his throttle full on, brought up the tail and held it off. The pursuit plane gathered speed. It stabbed upward, came around in a dangerous climbing turn and streaked after Barin.

Five hundred thousand pounds was quite worth fighting over, thought Pete. But there was more to it than that. Twice Barin had caught Pete with machine-gun fire in a defenseless ship. Twice Pete's airmanship had been humbled and bettered. Pete vowed it would not happen again.

Maybe he had been traveling just from New York to Washington and Washington to New York. Maybe he had thought that flying was just another job. But he was damned if anybody was going to come over to the United States and show up the ace of the ACA fleet, transport pilot or no.

CHAPTER NINE

Bullets Rip Through Wings

B ARIN saw that he would have to make a fight for it. Nothing loath, even anxious to down the man who had almost brought about his ruin, Barin verticaled and streaked back across the sky toward the oncoming pursuit plane.

Barin was confident. Master of flying and air fighting, his boast was that no man alive could best him in the air. Sleek and suave, a cold and heartless killer, he knew that he had nothing to fear at the hands of a transport pilot.

They exchanged shots at a range of a thousand yards and bored in.

Barin fired short bursts, stripping fabric from the pursuit plane's right wing. Pete banked to the right, offering a fair target for an instant. Barin raked the fuselage with smoking tracer.

Pete pulled up, went over on his back and rolled out of it. The world rocked crazily, the sea upended and threatened to spill out its brine. The sand dunes and surf and sky all tangled together.

Righted again, Pete expected to find himself on Barin's tail. He was not. Barin was angling in from the left, ripping at the red, white and blue fins with long bursts.

"Damn you," shouted Pete into the slipstream.

Barin fired short bursts, stripping fabric from the pursuit plane's right wing.

The pursuit ship swerved, verticaled and charged, engine screaming, guns going, eating up the sky.

Pete roared straight at Barin. For a split second, collision seemed inevitable. Barin broke and dived. Pete went over him, looped, rolled out of the top and streaked down upon Barin's tail.

Pete touched his trips. A score of rounds spattered into the black ship's rudders. Barin banked into a vertical. Pete followed him in.

They went around twice in a tight circle, with Pete striving to tighten it just enough to rake Barin's cockpit.

But Barin was schooled in the ways of war. He executed a Split-S, set his ship back on its tail and fired.

Pete overshot. Streamers of fabric fluttered from the hit left wing of the pursuit ship.

Swearing into the engines' snarl, Pete dived, looped and came back with everything on the fire.

Again a collision was only a matter of seconds. Barin tried to hold it. Boring straight at each other at hundreds of miles an hour, spinning prop face to face with spinning prop, neither of them would break.

Pete pressed his triggers. The butt of the cowl gun shivered. Brass shells poured, smoking, into the slipstream and over the side.

The distance narrowed to a hundred feet.

Flame rapped through Barin's prop, as his bullets probed for the pursuit ship.

Abruptly Barin faltered and swerved to the right. His club shattered into a thousand yowling fragments, fairly struck.

Pete lanced to his own right. Wing grazed wing.

The black ship was in a steep sideslip. Black smoke poured greasily out from under the cowl.

"Oh my God," wailed Pete. "The check!"

The black ship was going down in great, sickening swoops, starting long arcs and never finishing them, marking its fall with a mounting pillar of ugly smoke.

Barin was lolling over the side of the cockpit, his arms dangling toward the earth he would reach soon. In this war and that, he had hovered, gloating, over other men who went hurtling to death in flames. He was dying by the sword by which he had lived.

The black ship struck in the dunes. Scorching fragments soared skyward and slowly dropped back again. Crackling flame leaped up and ate away the fabric, showing the skeleton of tube steel.

Pete landed on the beach. He felt no elation of victory. The taking of revenge had not been very sweet for him, and now he had to force himself to approach the pyre.

He could not get within a hundred yards of the place, so great was the heat, and he walked around it in a wide circle, staring at it.

And then he found Barin.

The man had been thrown out of his cockpit by the impact. He lay sprawled on the sand, half buried by it, eyes hard and glazed, mouth gaping at the afternoon sky.

The black jacket was not scorched. In the pocket Pete found the check.

He was sorry that he had found it. In a way, the check was

his enemy. He had carried it without knowing that he had. It had brought him trouble in plenty, and now it had brought Barin death. It was, in fact, five hundred thousand pounds' worth of death itself.

It had brought the princess to him, and now it would take her away.

Dejectedly, Pete went back to the beach and taxied his pursuit ship up toward the shack and the waiting group.

When he arrived, the Coast Guard officer said, "Boy, that was some fight."

Duffy said, "Gee!"

The princess thanked Pete in a low voice.

Lady Louise said, harshly, "Did you get the check?"

Pete gave it over to the princess. "I suppose you'll be wanting to finish your trip to New York now," said Pete. "These gentlemen will take care of the rest of it."

She looked at him, puzzled.

He added, bitterly, "I've seen you through this far, Your Highness, I'll see you the rest of the way. I'll get you to New York and the Winton Arms Company just as soon as possible and . . ." He turned away to inspect Number Ten.

CHAPTER TEN

Pete England, Ace Pilot

TWO weeks later Pete was back on his regular run.
He was slumped down in his seat aboard Number Sixteen,
scowling at the oil temperature which wouldn't come up on
Engine Three and the jumpy revs of Engine One.

His hand rested upon his four throttles.

"That was swell of Brainard," said Duffy, in the copilot seat.

"You mean his commendation for me?" growled Pete.

"Uh?" said Duffy. "No, I meant that silver service he gave
Mary and me for the wedding. Boy, that was some wedding,
wasn't it, Pete? Say, by the way, you must have left early."

"Yeah," said Pete, trying to avoid a touchy subject like
weddings.

"You ought to get married some day," said Duffy innocently.

"Shut up," said Pete. "Why the hell would I get married?
New York to Washington and Washington to New York is
good enough for me. We've got schedules to make."

There was a silence. The dispatcher was waiting to hand
the passengers into the ship for the northbound trip. Nothing
had changed, to all appearances, but plenty had changed for
Pete.

Nothing would ever be right to Pete again. Not fifteen
minutes before, he had read a news item saying that the Princess
Maritza, accompanied by Lady Louise Something-or-other,

had sailed for Rangaria, having completed some diplomatic negotiations about arms exportations or something of the sort.

She was gone.

Someday she'd marry a prince, and from that moment Pete conceived an unreasonable hatred for princes in general.

Not a word from her since that evening he had landed her at Newark. Maybe it was best, at that. A princess would never marry a pilot.

A hand touched his shoulder. Some damned passenger . . . He turned to see what was wanted, wondering why Dan hadn't told them whatever they wanted to know.

"My God!" cried Pete in a stunned voice.

Her Highness was standing just behind him, smiling at him.

"Hello, Pete," said the princess.

Pete reared out of his seat, stepped over it and grabbed her arms. But he was still scared she had just come to say goodbye.

"Before anything . . . happens," said the princess, "let me apologize for keeping everything from you. I had to do that, on my word of honor. Lady Louise would not hear of it—"

"Where is she?" said Pete, ungallantly. "Lead me to her."

"She's gone with the princess," said the princess.

Pete gaped at her.

"But I thought—" stuttered Pete.

"I'm not the Princess Maritza of Rangaria, Pete. I am a girl named Janice Edmund, a steno in the State Department. I was offered ten thousand dollars to take the place of the Princess Maritza and deliver that check to New York. The princess—the real princess—was afraid that Barin was in the country. The Lady Louise carried through. She was real. Barin did not know the Princess Maritza, because he had been exiled ever since she was ten years old. He knew she had been educated in England. Anyway, Pete, I took the job. I needed the cash. I got ten thousand and a bonus of five thousand for the job, and I didn't think it would be fair to keep it when you did all the work. So I came down here tonight with the check and I heard what you said to Duffy and . . . I understand, Pete."

He brushed the check aside. Pete England wasn't interested in checks. In a smothered way, he said, "What was your right name?"

"Janice Edmund."

"We'll change all that," said Pete. "The last part anyway. Right now we're going to New York. Just sit right there and I'll show you how fast I can get there, Princess."

"Okay, Pete."

Story Preview

NOW that you've just ventured through one of the captivating tales in the Stories from the Golden Age collection by L. Ron Hubbard, turn the page and enjoy a preview of *Red Death Over China*. Join American pilot John Hampton in a breathtaking tale set against the backdrop of China's civil war. On one side is Chiang Kai-shek and, on the other, the army of Mao Tse-tung. An immense and deciding battle is about to take place, and its outcome oddly lies in Hampton's hands.

Red Death Over China

JOHN HAMPTON patrolled the eastern shore of the Yellow River in a way as careless and slipshod as the rickety, ancient Bristol.

The Bristol had wandered in from faraway England, an outcast, and wandered without any destination more definite than old age.

John Hampton was little better than his ship. He had less color to him than the dun plains which reached interminably to the smoky foothills. He was an in-between—he stood for nothing definite, he cared about nothing, he knew nothing he wanted.

Even the puffballs of volley fire on the ground meant little to him. He knew that the southern soldiers did not have enough training to lead him his length. Faintly contemptuous, he looked down at the muddy banks of the Yellow River, and inland to occasional barricades crudely made of bagged sand and piled muck.

Far away, a growing dot against the saffron haze of the day, another plane was coming. It could not be a friend, as the Bristol was the only plane Mao possessed and John Hampton, such as he was, the only pilot.

A fight was in the offing. He knew that and did not greatly care. The Bristol was fleet enough to run away.

Southern soldiers on the ground had seen their ally on the wing. Impulsively they leaped up on their earthworks—bouncing gray dots, something less than human.

Behind John Hampton, a Lewis yammered. He turned and looked at his gunner and shook his head.

The gunner showed no surprise, neither did he show any tendency to obey. He was a wild-eyed little man with uncontrollable black hair which came out from under his oversize helmet and streaked back from his yellow face in the whipping wind.

Chou, the gunner, again depressed the muzzles of the Lewis guns and raked a barricade. He looked defiantly back at the foreign devil in the front pit.

John Hampton shrugged. The Lewis started up again. Leaping puffs of dust sprang up beyond the barricades. Bouncing gray dots scrambled backwards, falling into grotesque, shuddering heaps.

John Hampton looked at the oncoming plane and turned a bend in the stream, his plane's shadow flowing through the depths of the murky water. He could wait a little while. It would look better if he took a burst or two before he went away. Not that he cared whether or not he made any show but, after all, his gunner would talk. As nearly as possible, Hampton stuck to the middle ground of existence.

The other plane was getting big enough to distinguish its type. It was a two-seater, an observation plane, but more than a match for the Bristol.

Hampton cared little about that either.

The rattle of the Lewis guns annoyed him, but it was useless to tell his tail gunner to stop.

The Rolls was cruising and still had a few horses to spare. Hampton kept on his course. There would be nothing to report this day. There was never anything to report. Men died on both sides of the river but they were men in gray cotton and there was nobody to mourn their passing.

General Mao's CPVAJR Army was fighting with its back to the Great Wall and the Sinkiang Desert, outnumbered, out-armed, but not out-generaled. The great Chiang was making one last great push to wipe out his rebel generals forever. And now only the Yellow River's greasy flood intervened. The fanatical troops of Mao were low on food, clothing, ammunition, rifles, horses. . . . But they were holding out at the Yellow River, dying on the wintry plains of Shensi.

The two-seater roared forward into the fray, hungry prop chopping off the distance in a churning blaze of light.

John Hampton squared around in the front cockpit of the Bristol and shoved his throttle full out. The clanking Rolls trembled in its mounts. The ancient Bristol's wings shivered. The patched fuselage angled away.

Chou's twin Lewis guns rattled ferociously and the southern two-seater veered hastily off.

Hampton had taken the burst. Now he could go home. He touched rudder and stick and stood the Bristol around.

The two-seater executed a swift three-sixty. Bow guns going, it clamped itself to the Bristol's tail. Tracer ate up from the rudder toward the gunner's pit, gobbling small round holes which smoked in the slipstream.

Hampton verticaled, cocking his right wing down at the river's yellow face. Chou raked the two-seater from prop to rudder, his wide eyes alight with joy.

But the southern plane was not touched in any vital spot. Pilot and gunner, caring little about an ancient Bristol, swooped away and came back under the Bristol's belly.

Hampton kicked rudder. Chou was almost over the side with his guns. He fired short, rapping bursts downward into the other two-seater's nose.

The Bristol straightened out again. Hampton was once more heading toward his field, away from the river.

The southern ship scrambled for height, went over the hump and streaked down. Chou, leaning back against the rim of his pit, centered his sights on the two-seater's nose and again let drive.

Small round holes, gashed by southern bullets, crept up the tail, inch by inch. Chou held his shaking guns and shouted defiance into the shattered wind.

The holes came inevitably forward. Hampton verticaled away. The two-seater hung on. Chou's words rose to a shrill scream, audible even above the yowl of engines and guns. He was driving his bullets with every ounce of energy he possessed.

The two-seater followed around. Once more the yellow waters were under the Bristol's canted wings. Once more the southern slugs were eating into the Bristol's fabric, rapping steadily forward to the gunner's pit.

Chou leaned into his Lewis guns. His bullets were almost

gone. His target was never in place. But he yelled and defied the southern dogs to try their worst.

The slugs came up the turtleback, smoking as they riveted wood and steel.

Chou's last bullets were chattering out. The two-seater's prop was in his sights. The target was fair, coming straight on for an instant. Chou held on.

The southern slugs passed over the mount, drove black dots into the leather seat, into the floor, into the empty ammunition racks.

The southerner's prop exploded into a fanning pattern of fragments. Smoke swept out from under the two-seater's cowl. Chou was holding on.

The two-seater lurched and dived helpless into the yellow water, sending up a soaring column of dirty spray.

Chou grinned feebly. He raised his hand halfway. It dropped suddenly over the side and Chou sagged over the skyward pointing guns. A small, dark trickle ran out of his mouth and out of his sleeve, to blend together and match the scarlet of the red star on the Bristol's side. Chou grinned again. He coughed and tried to right himself. His head dropped limply to wobble against the bright steel of his gun mounts.

Hampton looked back and saw him. He knew nothing could be done. The two-seater was a scattered patchwork raft floating slowly down with the murky river. The sky was clear. The barricades on the eastern shore were once again dotted with puffs of volley fire. Chou's glazed eyes looked down and back at them, not caring now.

The wind had carried the fight far down the stream, across

many bends of the tortuous course. When Hampton spotted his position he saw that the closest way home was through enemy country.

But the two-seater was gone and even though his gunner was dead, as long as his motor continued to run there was nothing to be feared.

Hampton was shaken. It was a new experience for him. His life was such an even, listless plane. He had seen many men die and he did not really care. But Chou—he had known him.

To find out more about *Red Death Over China* and how you can obtain your copy, go to www.goldenagestories.com.

Glossary

STORIES FROM THE GOLDEN AGE *reflect the words and expressions used in the 1930s and 1940s, adding unique flavor and authenticity to the tales. While a character's speech may often reflect regional origins, it also can convey attitudes common in the day. So that readers can better grasp such cultural and historical terms, uncommon words or expressions of the era, the following glossary has been provided.*

---

aileron: a hinged flap on the trailing edge of an aircraft wing, used to control banking movements.

Alleghenies: Allegheny Mountains; a mountain range comprising the western part of the Appalachian Mountains. The range extends about 500 miles (805 km) from northern Pennsylvania to southwest Virginia.

Anacostia: a neighborhood located in the southeast area of Washington, DC. It is located east of the Anacostia River, which flows from Maryland into Washington, DC and joins the Potomac River. This area also contained a narrow plain along the river where the Navy's Anacostia Naval Air Station and the Army's Bolling Field resided, originally established respectively in 1917 and 1918.

beam: an early form of radio navigation using beacons to define navigational airways. A pilot flew for 100 miles guided by the beacon behind him and then tuned in the beacon ahead for the next 100 miles. The beacons transmitted two Morse code signals, the letter "A" and the letter "N." When the aircraft was centered on the airway, these two signals merged into a steady, monotonous tone. If the aircraft drifted off course to one side, the Morse code for the letter "A" could be faintly heard. Straying to the opposite side produced the "N" Morse code signal.

Bolling: Bolling Field; established in 1918, and named in honor of the first high-ranking air service officer killed in World War I. The Army's Bolling Field resided on the east bank of the Anacostia River sharing an open plain with the Navy's Anacostia Naval Air Station. Bolling served as a research and testing ground for new aviation equipment and its first mission provided aerial defense of the capital.

Bristol: two-seater fighter biplane of World War I, manufactured by the British and flown by the Royal Air Force until 1932.

Chiang: Chiang Kei-shek (1887–1975); served as leader of the Chinese Nationalist Party after the death of its founder in 1925. In 1927 civil war broke out between the Nationalist government and the Red Army led by Mao Tse-tung. In 1934 Chiang surrounded the Communists but they broke out and began their Great Heroic Trek. In 1949 the Communists gained control of the Chinese mainland and Chiang retreated to Taiwan where he established a government in exile.

club: airplane propeller.

cowl: the removable metal housing of an aircraft engine, often designed as part of the airplane's body, containing the cockpit, passenger seating and cargo but excluding the wings.

cowl gun: a gun installed inside the cowl (metal covering over the engine) of an airplane.

CPVAJRA: Chinese People's Vanguard Anti-Japanese Red Army.

D of C or **Department of Commerce:** the department of the US federal government that promotes and administers domestic and foreign commerce. In 1926, Congress passed an Air Commerce Act that gave the US Department of Commerce some regulation over air facilities, the authority to establish air traffic rules and the authority to issue licenses and certificates.

dihedral: the upward or downward inclination of an aircraft wing from true horizontal, which is a self-stabilizing feature in the wing design. As the plane rolls to one side, the lower part of the wing starts to get more lift and then brings itself back up.

fins: fixed vertical surfaces at the tail of an aircraft that give stability, and to which the rudders are attached.

.45 Colt: a .45-caliber automatic pistol manufactured by the Colt Firearms Company of Hartford, Connecticut. Colt was founded by Samuel Colt (1814–1862), who revolutionized the firearms industry.

G-men: government men; agents of the Federal Bureau of Investigation.

gow up: to make sticky or mess something up. From *gow,* meaning opium or sap; the sticky brown resin harvested from poppies. Used figuratively.

ground loop: a sharp horizontal turn made by an aircraft on the ground when taxiing, landing or taking off.

key: a hand-operated device used to transmit Morse code messages.

kite: an airplane.

lady-in-waiting: a lady who is in attendance upon a queen or princess.

Lewis: a gas-operated machine gun designed by US Army Colonel Isaac Newton Lewis in 1911. The gun weighed twenty-eight pounds, only about half as much as a typical medium machine gun. The lightness of the gun made it popular as an aircraft-mounted weapon, especially since the cooling effect of the high-speed air over the gun meant that the gun's cooling mechanisms could be removed, making the weapon even lighter.

Luger: a German semiautomatic pistol introduced before World War I and named after German firearms expert George Luger (1849–1923).

Mao: Mao Tse-tung (1893–1976); Chinese leader of the Communist Party of China, who defeated the Chinese Nationalist Party led by Chiang Kai-shek in the Chinese Civil War (1927–1950).

minstrel show end man: a man at each end of the line of performers in a minstrel show who engages in comic banter with the master of ceremonies. A minstrel show is a comic variety show presenting jokes, songs, dances and skits, usually by white actors in blackface.

office: cockpit of an aircraft.

Rolls: an aircraft engine built by Rolls-Royce, a British car and aero-engine manufacturing company founded in 1906.

rudder: a device used to steer ships or aircraft. A rudder is a flat plane or sheet of material attached with hinges to the craft's stern or tail. In typical aircraft, pedals operate rudders via mechanical linkages.

rumrunners: people or ships engaged in bringing prohibited liquor ashore or across a border.

Scheherazade: the female narrator of *The Arabian Nights,* who during one thousand and one adventurous nights saved her life by entertaining her husband, the king, with stories.

Shensi: a province of east central China; one of the earliest cultural and political centers of China and site of the conclusion of the Great Heroic Trek (also known as the Long March).

sideslip: (of an aircraft when excessively banked) to slide sideways, toward the center of the curve while in turning.

slipstream: the airstream pushed back by a revolving aircraft propeller.

smear: smash.

Split-S: one of the oldest air combat maneuvers used to disengage from combat. To execute a Split-S, the pilot rolls his aircraft inverted and then executes a half-loop, resulting in the aircraft flying level in the opposite direction.

stevedoring: loading or unloading of a vessel.

three points: three-point landing; an airplane landing in which the two main wheels and the nose wheel all touch the ground simultaneously.

tracer: a bullet or shell whose course is made visible by a trail of flames or smoke, used to assist in aiming.

turtleback: the part of the airplane behind the cockpit that is shaped like the back of a turtle.

volley fire: simultaneous artillery fire in which each piece is fired a specified number of rounds without regard to the other pieces, and as fast as accuracy will permit.

Western Front: term used during World War I and II to describe the "contested armed frontier" (otherwise known as "the front") between lands controlled by the Germans to the East and the Allies to the West in Europe. In World War I, both sides dug in along a meandering line of fortified trenches stretching from the coast of the North Sea, southward to the Swiss border that was the Western Front. This line remained essentially unchanged for most of the war. In 1918 the relentless advance of the Allied armies persuaded the German commanders that defeat was inevitable and the government was forced to request armistice.

wingover: also known as the Immelmann turn; an aerial maneuver named after World War I flying ace Max Immelmann. The pilot pulls the aircraft into a vertical climb, applying full rudder as the speed drops, then rolls the aircraft while pulling back slightly on the stick, causing the aircraft to dive back down in the opposite direction. It has become one of the most popular aerial maneuvers in the world.

Yellow River: the second longest river in China, flowing through the north central part of the country.

L. Ron Hubbard
in the Golden Age
of Pulp Fiction

In writing an adventure story
a writer has to know that he is adventuring
for a lot of people who cannot.
The writer has to take them here and there
about the globe and show them
excitement and love and realism.
As long as that writer is living the part of an
adventurer when he is hammering
the keys, he is succeeding with his story.

Adventuring is a state of mind.
If you adventure through life, you have a
good chance to be a success on paper.

Adventure doesn't mean globe-trotting,
exactly, and it doesn't mean great deeds.
Adventuring is like art.
You have to live it to make it real.

— *L. RON HUBBARD*

L. Ron Hubbard
and American
Pulp Fiction

B ORN March 13, 1911, L. Ron Hubbard lived a life at least as expansive as the stories with which he enthralled a hundred million readers through a fifty-year career.

Originally hailing from Tilden, Nebraska, he spent his formative years in a classically rugged Montana, replete with the cowpunchers, lawmen and desperadoes who would later people his Wild West adventures. And lest anyone imagine those adventures were drawn from vicarious experience, he was not only breaking broncs at a tender age, he was also among the few whites ever admitted into Blackfoot society as a bona fide blood brother. While if only to round out an otherwise rough and tumble youth, his mother was that rarity of her time—a thoroughly educated woman—who introduced her son to the classics of Occidental literature even before his seventh birthday.

But as any dedicated L. Ron Hubbard reader will attest, his world extended far beyond Montana. In point of fact, and as the son of a United States naval officer, by the age of eighteen he had traveled over a quarter of a million miles. Included therein were three Pacific crossings to a then still mysterious Asia, where he ran with the likes of Her British Majesty's agent-in-place

L. Ron Hubbard, left, at Congressional Airport, Washington, DC, 1931, with members of George Washington University flying club.

for North China, and the last in the line of Royal Magicians from the court of Kublai Khan. For the record, L. Ron Hubbard was also among the first Westerners to gain admittance to forbidden Tibetan monasteries below Manchuria, and his photographs of China's Great Wall long graced American geography texts.

Upon his return to the United States and a hasty completion of his interrupted high school education, the young Ron Hubbard entered George Washington University. There, as fans of his aerial adventures may have heard, he earned his wings as a pioneering barnstormer at the dawn of American aviation. He also earned a place in free-flight record books for the longest sustained flight above Chicago. Moreover, as a roving reporter for *Sportsman Pilot* (featuring his first professionally penned articles), he further helped inspire a generation of pilots who would take America to world airpower.

Immediately beyond his sophomore year, Ron embarked on the first of his famed ethnological expeditions, initially to then untrammeled Caribbean shores (descriptions of which would later fill a whole series of West Indies mystery-thrillers). That the Puerto Rican interior would also figure into the future of Ron Hubbard stories was likewise no accident. For in addition to cultural studies of the island, a 1932–33

LRH expedition is rightly remembered as conducting the first complete mineralogical survey of a Puerto Rico under United States jurisdiction.

There was many another adventure along this vein: As a lifetime member of the famed Explorers Club, L. Ron Hubbard charted North Pacific waters with the first shipboard radio direction finder, and so pioneered a long-range navigation system universally employed until the late twentieth century. While not to put too fine an edge on it, he also held a rare Master Mariner's license to pilot any vessel, of any tonnage in any ocean.

Yet lest we stray too far afield, there is an LRH note at this juncture in his saga, and it reads in part:

"I started out writing for the pulps, writing the best I knew, writing for every mag on the stands, slanting as well as I could."

Capt. L. Ron Hubbard in Ketchikan, Alaska, 1940, on his Alaskan Radio Experimental Expedition, the first of three voyages conducted under the Explorers Club flag.

To which one might add: His earliest submissions date from the summer of 1934, and included tales drawn from true-to-life Asian adventures, with characters roughly modeled on British/American intelligence operatives he had known in Shanghai. His early Westerns were similarly peppered with details drawn from personal experience. Although therein lay a first hard lesson from the often cruel world of the pulps. His first Westerns were soundly rejected as lacking the authenticity of a Max Brand yarn (a particularly frustrating comment given L. Ron Hubbard's Westerns came straight from his Montana homeland, while Max Brand was a mediocre New York poet named Frederick Schiller Faust, who turned out implausible six-shooter tales from the terrace of an Italian villa).

Nevertheless, and needless to say, L. Ron Hubbard persevered and soon earned a reputation as among the most publishable names in pulp fiction, with a ninety percent placement rate of first-draft manuscripts. He was also among the most prolific, averaging between seventy and a hundred thousand words a month. Hence the rumors that L. Ron Hubbard had redesigned a typewriter for faster keyboard action and pounded out manuscripts on a continuous roll of butcher paper to save the precious seconds it took to insert a single sheet of paper into manual typewriters of the day.

That all L. Ron Hubbard stories did not run beneath said byline is yet another aspect of pulp fiction lore. That is, as publishers periodically rejected manuscripts from top-drawer authors if only to avoid paying top dollar, L. Ron Hubbard and company just as frequently replied with submissions under various pseudonyms. In Ron's case, the list

A MAN OF MANY NAMES

Between 1934 and 1950, L. Ron Hubbard authored more than fifteen million words of fiction in more than two hundred classic publications. To supply his fans and editors with stories across an array of genres and pulp titles, he adopted fifteen pseudonyms in addition to his already renowned L. Ron Hubbard byline.

Winchester Remington Colt
Lt. Jonathan Daly
Capt. Charles Gordon
Capt. L. Ron Hubbard
Bernard Hubbel
Michael Keith
Rene Lafayette
Legionnaire 148
Legionnaire 14830
Ken Martin
Scott Morgan
Lt. Scott Morgan
Kurt von Rachen
Barry Randolph
Capt. Humbert Reynolds

included: Rene Lafayette, Captain Charles Gordon, Lt. Scott Morgan and the notorious Kurt von Rachen—supposedly on the lam for a murder rap, while hammering out two-fisted prose in Argentina. The point: While L. Ron Hubbard as Ken Martin spun stories of Southeast Asian intrigue, LRH as Barry Randolph authored tales of

L. Ron Hubbard, circa 1930, at the outset of a literary career that would finally span half a century.

romance on the Western range—which, stretching between a dozen genres is how he came to stand among the two hundred elite authors providing close to a million tales through the glory days of American Pulp Fiction.

In evidence of exactly that, by 1936 L. Ron Hubbard was literally leading pulp fiction's elite as president of New York's American Fiction Guild. Members included a veritable pulp hall of fame: Lester "Doc Savage" Dent, Walter "The Shadow" Gibson, and the legendary Dashiell Hammett—to cite but a few.

Also in evidence of just where L. Ron Hubbard stood within his first two years on the American pulp circuit: By the spring of 1937, he was ensconced in Hollywood, adopting a Caribbean thriller for Columbia Pictures, remembered today as *The Secret of Treasure Island.* Comprising fifteen thirty-minute episodes, the L. Ron Hubbard screenplay led to the most profitable matinée serial in Hollywood history. In accord with Hollywood culture, he was thereafter continually called

The 1937 Secret of Treasure Island, *a fifteen-episode serial adapted for the screen by L. Ron Hubbard from his novel,* Murder at Pirate Castle.

upon to rewrite/doctor scripts—most famously for long-time friend and fellow adventurer Clark Gable.

In the interim—and herein lies another distinctive chapter of the L. Ron Hubbard story—he continually worked to open Pulp Kingdom gates to up-and-coming authors. Or, for that matter, anyone who wished to write. It was a fairly unconventional stance, as markets were already thin and competition razor sharp. But the fact remains, it was an L. Ron Hubbard hallmark that he vehemently lobbied on behalf of young authors—regularly supplying instructional articles to trade journals, guest-lecturing to short story classes at George Washington University and Harvard, and even founding his own creative writing competition. It was established in 1940, dubbed the Golden Pen, and guaranteed winners both New York representation and publication in *Argosy*.

But it was John W. Campbell Jr.'s *Astounding Science Fiction* that finally proved the most memorable LRH vehicle. While every fan of L. Ron Hubbard's galactic epics undoubtedly knows the story, it nonetheless bears repeating: By late 1938, the pulp publishing magnate of Street & Smith was determined to revamp *Astounding Science Fiction* for broader readership. In particular, senior editorial director F. Orlin Tremaine called for stories with a stronger *human element*. When acting editor John W. Campbell balked, preferring his spaceship-driven tales,

Tremaine enlisted Hubbard. Hubbard, in turn, replied with the genre's first truly *character-driven* works, wherein heroes are pitted not against bug-eyed monsters but the mystery and majesty of deep space itself—and thus was launched the Golden Age of Science Fiction.

The names alone are enough to quicken the pulse of any science fiction aficionado, including LRH friend and protégé, Robert Heinlein, Isaac Asimov, A. E. van Vogt and Ray Bradbury. Moreover, when coupled with LRH stories of fantasy, we further come to what's rightly been described as the foundation of every modern tale of horror: L. Ron Hubbard's immortal *Fear*. It was rightly proclaimed by Stephen King as one of the very few works to genuinely warrant that overworked term "classic"—as in: *"This is a classic tale of creeping, surreal menace and horror. . . . This is one of the really, really good ones."*

L. Ron Hubbard, 1948, among fellow science fiction luminaries at the World Science Fiction Convention in Toronto.

To accommodate the greater body of L. Ron Hubbard fantasies, Street & Smith inaugurated *Unknown*—a classic pulp if there ever was one, and wherein readers were soon thrilling to the likes of *Typewriter in the Sky* and *Slaves of Sleep* of which Frederik Pohl would declare: *"There are bits and pieces from Ron's work that became part of the language in ways that very few other writers managed."*

And, indeed, at J. W. Campbell Jr.'s insistence, Ron was regularly drawing on themes from the Arabian Nights and so introducing readers to a world of genies, jinn, Aladdin and Sinbad—all of which, of course, continue to float through cultural mythology to this day.

At least as influential in terms of post-apocalypse stories was L. Ron Hubbard's 1940 *Final Blackout*. Generally acclaimed as the finest anti-war novel of the decade and among the ten best works of the genre ever authored—here, too, was a tale that would live on in ways few other writers

imagined. Hence, the later Robert Heinlein verdict: "Final Blackout *is as perfect a piece of science fiction as has ever been written.*"

Like many another who both lived and wrote American pulp adventure, the war proved a tragic end to Ron's sojourn in the pulps. He served with distinction in four theaters and was highly decorated for commanding corvettes in the North Pacific. He was also grievously wounded in combat, lost many a close friend and colleague and thus resolved to say farewell to pulp fiction and devote himself to what it had supported these many years—namely, his serious research.

Portland, Oregon, 1943; L. Ron Hubbard captain of the US Navy subchaser PC 815.

But in no way was the LRH literary saga at an end, for as he wrote some thirty years later, in 1980:

"Recently there came a period when I had little to do. This was novel in a life so crammed with busy years, and I decided to amuse myself by writing a novel that was pure science fiction."

That work was *Battlefield Earth: A Saga of the Year 3000*. It was an immediate *New York Times* bestseller and, in fact, the first international science fiction blockbuster in decades. It was not, however, L. Ron Hubbard's magnum opus, as that distinction is generally reserved for his next and final work: The 1.2 million word *Mission Earth*.

> **Final Blackout**
> *is as perfect a piece of science fiction as has ever been written.*
>
> —Robert Heinlein

How he managed those 1.2 million words in just over twelve months is yet another piece of the L. Ron Hubbard legend. But the fact remains, he did indeed author a ten-volume *dekalogy* that lives in publishing history for the fact that each and every volume of the series was also a *New York Times* bestseller.

Moreover, as subsequent generations discovered L. Ron Hubbard through republished works and novelizations of his screenplays, the mere fact of his name on a cover signaled an international bestseller. . . . Until, to date, sales of his works exceed hundreds of millions, and he otherwise remains among the most enduring and widely read authors in literary history. Although as a final word on the tales of L. Ron Hubbard, perhaps it's enough to simply reiterate what editors told readers in the glory days of American Pulp Fiction:

He writes the way he does, brothers, because he's been there, seen it and done it!

THE STORIES FROM THE
GOLDEN AGE

Your ticket to adventure starts here with the Stories from
the Golden Age collection by master storyteller L. Ron Hubbard.
These gripping tales are set in a kaleidoscope of exotic locales and brim
with fascinating characters, including some of the
most vile villains, dangerous dames and brazen heroes
you'll ever get to meet.

The entire collection of over one hundred and fifty stories is being
released in a series of eighty books and audiobooks.
For an up-to-date listing of available titles,
go to www.goldenagestories.com.

AIR ADVENTURE

Arctic Wings	*Man-Killers of the Air*
The Battling Pilot	*On Blazing Wings*
Boomerang Bomber	*Red Death Over China*
The Crate Killer	*Sabotage in the Sky*
The Dive Bomber	*Sky Birds Dare!*
Forbidden Gold	*The Sky-Crasher*
Hurtling Wings	*Trouble on His Wings*
The Lieutenant Takes the Sky	*Wings Over Ethiopia*

FAR-FLUNG ADVENTURE

The Adventure of "X"
All Frontiers Are Jealous
The Barbarians
The Black Sultan
Black Towers to Danger
The Bold Dare All
Buckley Plays a Hunch
The Cossack
Destiny's Drum
Escape for Three
Fifty-Fifty O'Brien
The Headhunters
Hell's Legionnaire
He Walked to War
Hostage to Death

Hurricane
The Iron Duke
Machine Gun 21,000
Medals for Mahoney
Price of a Hat
Red Sand
The Sky Devil
The Small Boss of Nunaloha
The Squad That Never Came Back
Starch and Stripes
Tomb of the Ten Thousand Dead
Trick Soldier
While Bugles Blow!
Yukon Madness

SEA ADVENTURE

Cargo of Coffins
The Drowned City
False Cargo
Grounded
Loot of the Shanung
Mister Tidwell, Gunner

The Phantom Patrol
Sea Fangs
Submarine
Twenty Fathoms Down
Under the Black Ensign

110

TALES FROM THE ORIENT

MYSTERY

FANTASY

Borrowed Glory	*If I Were You*
The Crossroads	*The Last Drop*
Danger in the Dark	*The Room*
The Devil's Rescue	*The Tramp*
He Didn't Like Cats	

SCIENCE FICTION

The Automagic Horse	*A Matter of Matter*
Battle of Wizards	*The Obsolete Weapon*
Battling Bolto	*One Was Stubborn*
The Beast	*The Planet Makers*
Beyond All Weapons	*The Professor Was a Thief*
A Can of Vacuum	*The Slaver*
The Conroy Diary	*Space Can*
The Dangerous Dimension	*Strain*
Final Enemy	*Tough Old Man*
The Great Secret	*240,000 Miles Straight Up*
Greed	*When Shadows Fall*
The Invaders	

WESTERN

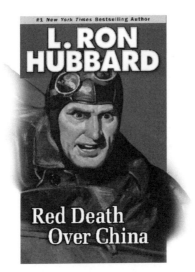